Tales From The Spired Inn

Tales From The Spired Inn

Stephen Palmer

NewCon Press
England

First edition, published in the UK October 2019
by NewCon Press

NCP 216 (hardback)
NCP 217 (softback)

10 9 8 7 6 5 4 3 2 1

ISBN: 978-1-912950-41-6 (hardback)
978-1-912950-42-3 (softback)

Cover art by Stephen Palmer
Cover layout by Stephen Palmer and Ian Whates

Edited by Ian Whates
Interior layout by Storm Constantine

Contents

Introduction

Memory Seed began with lots of long walks.

It was 1988. I was living in Surrey at the time, having left university just up the A30 five years earlier, and nearby lay the green spaces of Virginia Water and Windsor Great Park – part manicured, part wild. On my many walks I'd think about the novels I was writing, or planning to write. One day, a couple of years after I'd written my first attempt at a novel, I was inspired by the greenery to think about a scenario where a coastal city was surrounded by, and then invaded by rampant vegetation. I had two mental images: one of a series of moss-covered roofs leading down to the sea, the other of a high class bordello that was a cover for some other operation. Later I imagined characters who might inhabit this city, which, after the supercomputer, I named Kray (for some reason I imagined a supercomputer at the heart of the place). This novel, I knew, would have a strong environmental theme. Soon the characters and scenario began to grow wild in my imagination.

The first draft wasn't great so I put it aside, but four years later I was inspired to return to the scenario – the first time I'd ever done that. Something in Kray called me back. The second draft was much better, and, excited and reinvigorated, I began sending the first three chapters and a synopsis around to publishers. Nobody bit.

But then random chance stepped in to aid me. It turned out that somebody at Orbit Books had read the chapters and been deeply struck by them. At the end of 1993, just days before I moved house, he wrote to me. (Had I moved even a week earlier I would never have received that letter!) But by 1994 I had a third version of the novel prepared, and this I sent back to Orbit. The year passed by. I gave up hope. Then, at the end of the year, I was told there was a chance my novel would be accepted for publication. A couple of months later, it was.

Needless to say, I was gobsmacked. Much later I discovered the odds against being plucked from the slush pile – had I known those odds I might never have bothered sending my chapters around the London publishing companies. But I did get lucky all those years ago, and a while later my debut was published under the title *Memory Seed* (a title we had to come up with just weeks before the deadline, and which a friend, suggesting Seeds Of Memory, created for me).

The novel encapsulates all my early interests and influences, some of which I have retained. There is a strong green theme – the Earth fighting back against a self-centred humanity which has ruined it. Almost all the characters are women – I had been a committed feminist since my mid-twenties. There is a sense of enigma and gothic mystery encouraged by my love of Gene Wolfe's books, matched with my vivid imagination, which for some readers recalled Jack Vance. All in all, I was told, this was a striking combination, and later on reviews confirmed this.

In later years I wrote three short stories, linking them to the Spired Inn, inside which, at the start of the novel, Zinina begins her actions against Kray's Citadel rulers. The Spired Inn epitomised Kray for me; that combination of ancient tradition, modern technology, weird neighbours and peculiar clientele.

To this day Kray intrigues me. A few years ago I acquired the rights to the novel from Orbit, but by then all digital copies of the novel had been lost, so I had to buy a paperback copy, tear each page out to OCR scan it, then reassemble the text in Word. Because of that process, I read the novel and gave it a light edit, finding the qualities of the place still mesmerising: the plants, the people, the rain, the strange societies, the sense of doom and regret. The atmosphere of Kray represents me in

a deep way. So I was delighted when, completely out of the
blue, Ian Whates asked me to write two new *Tales From The
Spired Inn* for this collection.

It really has been marvellous to smell the reeking air and
feel that warm rain once again…

Stephen Palmer
Shropshire
November 2018

Dr Vanchovy's Final Case

Good evening. My name is Barakystys, and I work the evening shift behind the bar at the Spired Inn. I work every day, come storm, rain or drizzle. It is bearable toil.

The tale I am about to tell is one of murder and detection in this final year of humanity on Earth, when all is madness and chaos – bladder blade plants kill the unwary, youngsters are surprised by falling cushions of fungus, cats with silicon implants in their claws prowl the streets for prey. And there are gang wars, street battles, and feuds settled by high energy rifles. For we are told by the demagogues, by the priestesses of the Goddess, in fact by *everybody*, that the long despoliation of the planet is over and the Earth is fighting back.

We who live and work in the northern half of the city of Kray are perhaps more used to death than soft southerners. Most of us do not consider the question of whether the killing of a human being still counts as murder. So what if somebody gets murdered? Should we still care?

This tale of mine may help you decide that question.

It was about Eostre time when the deed was done. Early awakening trees were soft with orange and yellow blossom. From rusting cable cars long strings of deadly moss hung; they looked like sticky ropes, dotted with the bodies of entangled insects. There was an eerie beauty in the world, and many were the times I wandered the main streets of the Carmine Quarter, more for melancholy pleasure than any other purpose. I walked alone. All my family died last winter.

On the evening of the murder the Spired Inn was quiet. There had been a furious battle between reveller tribes and laser-toting teenagers from the Temple of Youth, and so the streets around the Inn, so close to the Cemetery, were empty. Several people sat drinking smart dooch in the common room. I remember the aamlon twins, Praes-lin and Daes-lin, playing chess. Also there was Dr Vanchovy, the famous detective and noted dandy, and Aqa the belly-dancer and her percussionist friend Jizhaqar. I suppose I should mention here the victim of this tale, Yasque, a drifter formerly employed as doorwoman to the Temple of the Goddess. Who was she? It is difficult to say. She did odd jobs for odd people. She was a loner, a tart.

On the night of the murder, all these people were drinking at the Spired Inn. I was behind the bar with Dhow-lin, the owner. Because it was quiet I spent a lot of time chatting with the clientele, especially Dr Vanchovy, who only popped in occasionally, and Aqa, who I was trying to bed. Dr Vanchovy was in an expansive mood, and he bought me a drink, and one for Aqa, and Yasque too. As usual his dress was clean and perfect, excepting the eye patch that he had recently taken to wearing over his artificial eye. It must have been uncomfortable because he kept adjusting it. He talked with Yasque early in the evening. I remember she wore tattered clothes and a tribal necklace of small globes. With me he discussed the healing properties of oils derived from the organs of genetically engineered fish.

The other main character in this drama was Baylockell, a dour man recently expelled from the Temple of Pure Justice. At the time he was living in a house off the alley behind the inn, with his sister. He came in a few times a week.

Early in the evening Yasque went to the room on the first floor that she was renting. Nobody ever spoke to her again.

It was Dhow-lin who discovered her body, one hour before midnight. Crying and making a fuss, she ran down to the common room and shouted, "There's been a killing! Here! Curse all Krayans. A killing, in *my* inn."

Of course, everybody took notice. Immediately Dr Vanchovy stood up and said, "Leave this to me. I shall use my detective skills to elicit the circumstances of the case. Dhow-lin, you must see to it that nobody leaves." He was like that, Dr Vanchovy, a bit formal when it came to public speaking. I tried not to laugh as he examined himself in a handy mirror and brushed down his beige jacket.

Dhow-lin was angry. "You can rely on me to do that," she said.

I walked with Dr Vanchovy to the room on the first floor, Dhow-lin muttering behind us.

Poor Yasque – I felt sorry for her now – lay stretched out on her mess of a bed, neck exposed and head flung back, a rough blanket covering the rest of her body. As Dhow-lin and Dr Vanchovy surveyed the room, I tip-toed over to her body, for I had seen a slip of white neoprene in her hand. I took it and said, "Look, she wrote a note to somebody."

Immediately Dr Vanchovy said, "Put that down, boy! You are contaminating the evidence."

But it was too late. I had read it. It said:

You will never get it. That's final. Stop hounding me.

Dr Vanchovy snatched the slip from me, a black expression on his face. Dhow-lin scolded me, saying, "Can't you keep your fingers to yourself, boy?"

"Sorry," I said. Secretly, I was wondering who Yasque's nuisance admirer might be. She bedded mostly men, I knew. Anybody, really, if they paid.

I watched as Dr Vanchovy examined the body. He slipped a few bits and pieces into his pocket, including the necklace of small globes, then led us back to the common room. There he solemnly addressed us.

"Yasque has been poisoned. Now then, I notice that our two famous chess players can see the steps up to the corridor on the first floor. Praes-lin, who have you seen go that way this evening?"

Praes-lin scratched a flea bite on her arm then replied, "Only three. Jizhaqar went up there, and later Aqa. And Baylockell. He went up there last of all."

Dr Vanchovy nodded. "Then we have three suspects, and one of them is sure to be the murderer. Aqa the belly dancer, Jizhaqar the tambourine player, and Baylockell, lately of the Temple of Pure Justice. Tomorrow morning I shall begin my investigation."

"What shall we do with these suspects tonight?" asked Dhow-lin.

Dr Vanchovy turned to me. "Boy, run along and request doorwomen from the Temple of the Goddess. They will ensure nobody escapes the inn." He turned to a frowning Dhow-lin to add, "Yasque once worked there, so they will agree."

I could not help it. I had to speak out. "But what of the note?" I wanted to be part of the investigation.

Dr Vanchovy frowned and said, "Leave the question of the note to me."

He looked very much the professional detective bothered by a serving boy. I blushed, and lowered my gaze to the ground.

It is now time to tell of the events that followed the discovery of the victim.

The Temple of the Goddess could spare only three doorwomen. Two guarded the front and rear doors of the inn while the third watched the upper floor windows. It was not ideal, but at least they were wearing light-amplifying contact lenses.

To my surprise, Dr Vanchovy instructed me to guard the room where the body lay all night, and under no circumstances to let anybody in. Even Dhow-lin was banned. I racked my brain as to why I should have to perform this onerous task, deciding that because too few doorwomen had arrived I was to be an extra line of security. In fact my brain was active all night, as I pondered who might have killed poor Yasque, the drifter so lost in this terrible city. You can be sure that I came to no conclusion.

When Dr Vanchovy returned next morning I slept for a few hours, while he prepared the common room for the interrogation of the suspects. Before he began he paid a visit to the scene of the crime. Hunched over, he searched the drapes at the window, at length uttering a muted cry and bending down to push his right hand under the couch there.

"So!" he said. He pulled out an intricate knife with a needle-like blade and a twirled handle. Immediately I recognised it as typical of poisoned stilettos used by priests of the Temple of Pure Justice.

"Baylockell was here," I gasped.

"Yes, my boy," replied Dr Vanchovy. "I think he is to be my main suspect."

Holding the knife between thumb and forefinger he approached Yasque's body and peered at the neck, before touching the blade to her, just below the ear.

"An exact fit," he remarked. "Come downstairs, boy. With your estimable employer Dhow-lin we will begin the interrogations."

This we did. The four of us sat in the common room. To be frank, I was excited, but nervous also. I hardly knew Yasque. It was the skill of Dr Vanchovy and the inexorable progress of the deductions that amazed me. I watched as he preened himself like a perfumed peacock; the eyepatch had gone. But how I wanted to be a detective that morning!

We had cleared the room so that none would hear any intimate details. I was the official recorder, taping the conversations onto a bio-rec. Baylockell frowned throughout the interview. He was a tall man, moustached, sallow, with dark eyes and a serious expression. As befitted a former man of the Temple of Pure Justice he showed no emotion, nor any real interest in the proceedings. He just answered mechanically.

"Baylockell," Dr Vanchovy began, "do you recognise this knife?"

"It is from the Temple of Pure Justice."

"Yes. So I thought. This knife was found under a drape at the windowed end of Yasque's chamber. Can you shed any light upon how it might have got there?"

"No," Baylockell answered.

"Would you agree that it acts as evidence against you?"

"Circumstantial evidence, maybe. But I did not enter Yasque's room, nor have I ever seen that knife."

"So you say," Dr Vanchovy said, leaning forward.

"Anybody could have entered Yasque's room by the window."

"The window was locked and has not been forced. For somebody to enter, force would have been necessary."

"So you say."

Dr Vanchovy tried another tack. "A note was found in Yasque's hand. It tells of a lover who was forcing himself upon her. You, perhaps."

"No. Yasque was a cheap floozy who slept only with customers. I have never sullied myself with her."

Dr Vanchovy sat back as if estimating the tolerance of his suspect. His eyes narrowed in an overly theatrical gesture. "I put it to you," he said, "that you had been forcing your attentions upon the unfortunate Yasque, and when she refused you, telling you to stop hounding her, you poisoned her with your temple knife."

"Nonsense," said Baylockell. It seems odd now, but he actually looked bored with the whole affair. I tried to guess his thoughts. He seemed guilty to me.

"Do you deny that you passed her door on the first floor corridor?" Dr Vanchovy asked.

"No."

"What were you doing in that corridor?"

Baylockell replied, "I went to visit a drugs merchant who was staying the night."

"Can you prove that?"

"Find the merchant and you will have your proof."

Dr Vanchovy turned to Dhow-lin. Before he had even asked his question she said, "Yes, there was a drugs vendor staying in a room off that corridor, Glaanijk-lin of the Mercantile Quarter."

"And where is she now?"

"She went to the south of the city," said Dhow-lin. "She told me she doubted she would return."

Dr Vanchovy frowned. "Convenient for you," he told Baylockell.

"Nevertheless," Baylockell replied, "she is my reason for walking past Yasque's room, and she will provide my alibi for the time I was not drinking in the common room."

Dr Vanchovy clicked his tongue. "A most unsatisfactory state of affairs. Very well, for the moment I am done with you."

I departed the common room, my work over for the time being.

It was then that I received a surprise. Who should accost me in the kitchen but Aqa, distressed, tears beginning to form in her eyes.

"What is it?" I asked.

She put her hand on my arm and replied, "Something awful has happened. Jizhaqar is in a terrible state."

"Why?"

"Because she entered Yasque's room last night, and she told me that Yasque was stretched out dead on her bed!"

Goddess! I had been told by my precious Aqa that Jizhaqar had seen Yasque dead before either Aqa or Baylockell had passed by. I was astonished. This could only mean that Jizhaqar was lying and had for some unknown reason killed Yasque. She had been the person who had planted the knife in order to implicate Baylockell.

I decided not to disturb Dr Vanchovy with my news. You must understand that this was in part because I had already angered him with my behaviour; but I also wanted to see how Jizhaqar would react under questioning.

First, however, it was Aqa's turn to be interrogated.

She was first asked, "Did you enter Yasque's room?"

"No, I didn't."

"But you did pass by?"

"Oh, yes," Aqa replied. "I go past that room every night to collect my dancing gear from the store room."

Dr Vanchovy turned to Dhow-lin and said, "Is this true?"

"Yes, it's true. Besides, Aqa has no motive. She liked Yasque."

Dr Vanchovy returned his gaze to Aqa and said, "For the moment I have no more questions. You are dismissed."

Then it was Jizhaqar's turn.

She was very nervous. A tall, lithe woman of about thirty, she seemed now a shrunken child, pale, with dark rings around her eyes. She almost tripped over as she made her way to the chair that stood opposite Dr Vanchovy.

"Now then," he began. "You were seen passing along the corridor off which Yasque's room lay. Is this true?"

"Yes."

"What were you doing there?"

Jizhaqar squirmed in her seat. "I can't remember exactly. I live here at the inn. I go as I please."

"Hmmm. And did you enter Yasque's room?"

"No."

I tried to conceal my shock at this answer. Jizhaqar did not know that Aqa had relayed to me what she had been told. Jizhaqar was lying to Dr Vanchovy, thinking that nobody in the common room would know otherwise. As you can imagine, my suspicions were immediately aroused. Yes, she told Aqa that she had found Yasque's body, but we had no proof of that. Jizhaqar could have lied to Aqa, as she had lied here. Also, as I sat there, my mind a buzz of thoughts, I recalled an incident between the two women in which Jizhaqar had angrily denounced Yasque as a drunkard. Could there have been a rift between the two, leading to the murder?

Dr Vanchovy was continuing his interrogation. I wanted to interrupt, but I dared not. It was at this point that I decided to undertake my own investigation. I too would be a detective.

That afternoon I spoke in secret with Aqa. To tell the truth I had a second motive, for I hoped we could form a stronger friendship, one that might even lead to a proper relationship. I would not say that I loved her, but she had certainly caught my eye… As would any belly dancer, I suppose.

In her boudoir we discussed the situation. I had never been there before, and at first found myself distracted by the glittery clothes and exotic perfumes arranged neatly about the place. Dr Vanchovy would have thought himself in heaven!

Aqa repeated what Jizhaqar had told her. "She said that she had gone into Yasque's room and seen the body lying on the bed, exactly as Dr Vanchovy described last night. She said she was scared, shocked, and that was why she failed to report what she had found. She did not want to approach the body. She hoped Yasque was just blind drunk."

"But why did she go into the room?" I asked.

"She didn't say. But I got the impression that she wanted to speak with Yasque."

"There is the matter of the note," I said. "I think it is the crux of this whole case." I moved close to Aqa, in a conspiratorial fashion. "We must do our own investigation. I've just seen Jizhaqar lie to Dr Vanchovy. She told him she never entered Yasque's room."

Aqa nodded. "There's something odd going on."

I continued, "The note was written in Yasque's hand, and said, 'You will never get it. That's final. Stop hounding me.' What could that mean?"

Aqa shrugged her lovely shoulders and said, "I don't know. Maybe Yasque possessed something owned by Jizhaqar."

I considered this. We had all interpreted the note as referring to matters of the bed, but perhaps that was a mistake. Also, what if Jizhaqar was telling the truth? Suppose somebody else murdered Yasque before the three suspects passed her room? But no. The chess-playing twins were adamant that they had only seen the three. Yet that implied the knife was an anomaly.

Earnestly I told Aqa, "I'm going to get to the bottom of this. If the murderer is one of the three suspects then that knife doesn't fit. Yes, it is a poisoned weapon, but that doesn't necessarily mean it was used to kill Yasque."

"Dr Vanchovy said she had been poisoned through a neck wound."

"Yes," I admitted. "But think, Aqa. Suppose you wanted to implicate someone else, for instance Baylockell? If you knew he would be drinking at the inn on the night of the murder, where would you go to get that type of knife?"

"The Temple itself."

"As will we. Come on!"

And so, like two excited children, we made our way east to the Temple of Pure Justice. That day the rain fell from an especially dark sky, so we took torches to find our way. The streets were a phantasm of lights and reflections, of neon and torchlight. How easy it was to imagine that this was indeed our last year, in the gloom, in the methanous stink, in the fecund vegetation of our crumbling city. How difficult it was to believe that beyond the walls of Kray no other human being stood on the face of the Earth, that all outside was deadly empty green.

It was during this walk that Aqa and I first held hands. You will not doubt me when I say my heart sang.

The Temple was a structure of bakelite and steel, all perpendicular lines and right angles, as severe and forbidding as the moral code of the priests inside. I quailed when I saw that it was guarded by seven-eared automata in the form of daemons. There was blood on their sabre teeth. One human guard faced us, an old man dressed in a long coat of felted luminous moss. He refused us entry to the temple because we could not demonstrate our ethical purity.

But I had an idea. From a wall screen I accessed the temple's diary, where they described the day's services, listed priests available and dispensed news.

"Look at today's news page," I said.

Aqa read it out. "Sacred knife stolen late last night or early this morning. Food reward for safe return."

"Don't you see?" I said. "The knife wasn't in Yasque's room last night. Somebody put it there this morning to implicate Baylockell. All we have to do is find out who slipped in before Dr Vanchovy found it and we have our murderer!"

What, then, had I learned so far?

Well, I knew that Jizhaqar had lied to Dr Vanchovy, and I knew that the knife from the Temple of Pure Justice had been placed in the room between my leaving guard duties for a well-earned sleep and Dr Vanchovy finding it. I also knew a note had been written by Yasque to some unknown person: *You will never get it. That's final. Stop hounding me.*

And that was about it.

To be frank with you, I was still confused at this point. If Jizhaqar had lied to Aqa then she would seem to be the most obvious candidate. On the other hand, if she was telling the truth, then somebody had murdered Yasque before the three suspects passed her door, an apparent impossibility. Jizhaqar, then, seemed to be our culprit.

If I could show that Jizhaqar had not been in her room that night when the knife was stolen, it would prove her guilt. Yet how could she have escaped the guarded inn? I considered the possibility that she already owned such a knife, but of course that was absurd. There had to be another explanation.

By now, it was time for Dr Vanchovy to bring us together in the common room and reveal who the murderer was. We all gathered, and I set up the bio-rec, plugging it into an analytical pyuter. Dr Vanchovy looked dapper in a powder-blue overall, and again I noticed he was no longer wearing an eyepatch, his infatuation with that particular fashion seemingly over. Dhowlin and the three suspects were also there. Of the latter, Jizhaqar looked petrified, Aqa seemed disorientated, while Baylockell was as calm as ever.

"I begin by pointing out the evidence," said Dr Vanchovy. "We have a victim, Yasque, who was poisoned. We have three suspects, all of whom had an opportunity to commit the murder. We have one main piece of evidence linking one of the suspects to the crime. This is what happened. On the night of the murder, Baylockell had an argument with Yasque over the affair he wished to conduct with her. She spurned his advances and he poisoned her, using the envenomed knife that he had carried since leaving the Temple of Pure Justice. In his fit, he hid the knife in the first available place, then departed."

Then I looked into Dr Vanchovy's artificial eye and had the answer.

I stood up. "No," I said in a clear voice.

Dr Vanchovy was too surprised to stop me from

continuing.

"I have something to say," I said.

Dr Vanchovy laughed. "I cannot fault your eagerness, boy." He waved me on. "Pray give us your version of events."

So I began my reconstruction of events on the night of the murder.

"Last night," I said, "Aqa and I went to the Temple of Pure Justice, where we discovered that a sacred knife had been stolen. It is my contention that the knife was placed in Yasque's room *after* I finished guard duty, long after the facts of Yasque's murder were known to us all in the Spired Inn. Now what I have been asking myself is this: why was the knife placed in the room so long after the murder? The answer is that the murderer must have realised it would be needed after Yasque had been found. It was needed in order to implicate someone else. Do you get my drift?"

"No," came the reply from several confused people.

"Yasque was not dead when Dhow-lin found her."

Silence.

"You must have a reason for saying that," Dhow-lin told me.

"I have," I assured her. "I believe the murderer did not initially intend to kill Yasque, but only to drug her, in order to reclaim an item owned by Yasque. This is what the note is about. It refers not to matters of the bed, but to an actual object. Yet something happened after the drugging that made Yasque's death necessary. What was that event, I wonder?"

"Wait," said Dr Vanchovy. "If Yasque was not dead when Dhow-lin found her, who murdered her afterwards? And more importantly, how?"

"This is what we all want to know," I replied.

Here, I left a dramatic pause.

After a moment Dr Vanchovy said, "Well?"

I looked at him and said, "You removed several items from

Yasque when you first examined the body. What were they?"

"Just trivial items of no importance," he replied.

"If they are so trivial," I said, "you will not mind detailing them."

"They are of no importance to my investigation. I merely removed them to gain some idea of Yasque's character."

"I think not, Dr Vanchovy. You removed them because you wanted them. One was the object referred to in the note, which I believe to have been her tribal necklace of many small globes."

He remained silent, but then frowned and said, "You trawl deep waters, boy."

"Listen to the rest of my theory," I said. "Earlier that evening Dr Vanchovy bought a drink for himself and one for Yasque. He drugged it, and she drank it. Later, she went to her room. Dr Vanchovy was surprised and annoyed when Dhowlin discovered what she thought was Yasque's body, because this upset his plans. Now Dr Vanchovy had to act quickly if he was to retrieve the object he so desired. He stood up and declared that he would undertake an investigation. We went to the room. But here my own innocent eagerness was to make his situation worse, for I discovered the note. Once I had read it, the contents of that note were public knowledge. It was only then that Dr Vanchovy decided to kill Yasque, so that she would not wake up and reveal a truth that would shame him. He had a little time to act. Yasque was still drugged, her pulse very slow, her breathing almost imperceptible. Nobody else had examined the body. So he had me stand guard – that she not be disturbed. Next morning, with the knife concealed in his sleeve, he and I entered the room, where he pretended to find the knife. Then he compared the blade with a mark he feigned finding on Yasque's neck. It was only *then* that he introduced the poison to her body. We were all dazzled by his brilliance. We did not think to question his procedures."

"This is all very well," said Dhow-lin, "but why was Yasque's tribal necklace so desired by Dr Vanchovy?"

"Isn't it obvious?" I replied. "What was the one thing marring his sartorial perfection? It was his eye-patch. Yasque wore his missing artificial eye around her neck – it was *part of the necklace*. As she stated in the private note that I made public, she refused to return it to him. Dr Vanchovy murdered her so that the shameful truth, that a tart wore his eye on her necklace, would never be revealed to us."

In a low voice Dr Vanchovy said, "Nonsense."

I turned to him. "Your intention was to remove your artificial eye then return the necklace to Yasque, wasn't it? If she had spoken up you would have scoffed at her, and everybody would have laughed at such an absurd story."

Dr Vanchovy stood up, but Dhow-lin produced a laser pistol and pointed it at him. "You will come with me," she said, "and we will arrange your future."

"My future?" he replied.

"I think the priestesses of the Goddess will accept you, Dr Vanchovy. They will rip off your fine clothes and dress you in rags, then dump you in a cell where you will remain, quite alone, until this city is green and dead."

Thus did the events surrounding Yasque's death come to their conclusion. We will probably never know how she first came into possession of Dr Vanchovy's artificial eye, but I hope you will agree when I say that he did a bad thing, an inhumane thing, taking the life of an innocent for such a trivial reason. He thought he would get away with it. He did not. In the end, human life is valuable even in circumstances as desperate as those of Kray.

So I conclude my tale from the Spired Inn. In this tale the detective did it, which explains why it was Dr Vanchovy's final case.

Funeral For A Pyuter

Qmeela was tipped off by Dhow-lin, the flea-bitten owner of the Spired Inn, that something unusual might happen at the funeral. Qmeela tried to extract more from the old aamlon, but failed. Dhow-lin shuffled her dusty vests and looked elsewhere, mouth shut.

Drowsy beside an open fire, Qmeela glanced across sea-fat candles to a clutch of luminous anjiqs, yellow with age, where sat the reveller contingent. The common room was a single area of oaken alcoves, cobwebs and dead lampshades hanging from the ceiling, a broad space now empty of others, except for some tail-wagging rats. The reveller presence made most locals nervous. Some had gone upstairs to play chess. Some had ventured out into the rain.

Dhow-lin coughed. "You'd better wake up, sly-girl. Granny looks like she's ready for the off."

Qmeela frowned. "Don't call me that."

"Ah, I'm only pulling your tail. You ain't no Zinina."

Qmeela paid no attention to the remark as the reveller group got to their feet and headed for the exit. Qmeela followed; and her heartbeat began to race. This was no ordinary funeral on no ordinary day. As the reveller grandmother glanced at her, she thought to herself: *I'm only here because I document reveller culture... unless Dhow-lin's warning concerns the dead thing itself...*

She paused in the green zone while the revellers pulled on their raincoats. Another thought occurred to her: *my mother helped to manufacture Majaq-Aqhaj... Could that be why granny wanted me to tag along to its funeral?* She watched as Fynessan and Liefferyny, the grandmother's aides, stuffed grilled fat into their mouths, washed it down with inn beer, then opened the door and threw out the tankards.

Qmeela followed as they walked out. Old custom: follow fermented juice, follow the path of barleycorn living, seed to beer to death. Six more revellers departed the inn, to crowd around the grandmother.

Outside, the rain had receded. Mists from the Cemetery loomed along Morte Street, while from the Carmine Quarter far below she heard the weird thrumming of the Cowhorn Tower's prongs. A nearby clock chimed twelve bells of noon. She glanced back at the aquamarine lanterns of the inn, then shuddered. This was it! The funeral itself.

The reveller grandmother looked at her, then grimaced. "What's the matter, dark one?" she asked. "Wanna go back to your hot burnin' logs?"

"No thank you," Qmeela replied.

The grandmother waved an algae-green finger at her. "You better not. You can get cosy afterwards, with that rodent-lover Dhow-lin. You said you'd write this up for your pyuter records."

"I will, Granny. For the Vert Day celebrations. So people won't forget you and the revellers."

The grandmother turned to her kin and said, "Pah! Dark-girl knows how to write. So what? Can she flock the meat off a defender in time for supper? Nah!"

Fynessan laughed, sending Qmeela a look of scorn, but Qmeela ignored it. She knew her place.

Liefferyny said, "But, Granny, does she *have* to come? She's only a no-bloom."

Qmeela held her breath. She began to tremble. Then she walked up to Liefferyny and said, "You take that back, sharpy. I'll slit —"

"Oy, oy!" cried the grandmother, raising her arms. "Calm it."

"I'm a fellow bedder," Qmeela told Liefferyny, "and just as entitled to be at this funeral as you are."

Liefferyny spat. Green gob landed at Qmeela's feet. "Only 'cos of your mother, and that ain't no decent call. That's knacky, that is, you gormless sop."

The reveller grandmother reached out to slap Liefferyny on the face. "I said *calm* it. Respect this day of Majaq-Aqhaj. Dark one's a half-bloom, see? Anyway, we got Youthmeat to deal with in a while, and that's not me spouting lichen slime."

Liefferyny inclined her face to the ground. "Yes, Granny. Sorry."

Qmeela looked away to take the pressure off the revellers, pretending to check the kit at her belt. They muttered to themselves, then moved off. Qmeela followed at a distance. So... her mother *was* the reason she had been told to attend the funeral.

The procession headed east into the mist, then hopped over a cord to enter the Cemetery. Soon Qmeela saw a great marquee of black canvas laid out between two stands of yew. At one side of the marquee a group of eight young women huddled beside a glowing statue, shielding themselves from the rain with shagreen umbrellas.

Liefferyny hissed. "They brought along their manky kid!" she cried.

The grandmother jabbed her in the ribs. "Ain't you learned nothing? This is a funeral of two halves. 'Course they're gonna bring their idol. It's to balance our Eskhthonatos."

"But they're Youthmeat... and it's *luminous.*"

"*Shut* it, shouster. That ain't no insult, not today anyway. Just support me like I told you to – mouth closed. We got to bear the unbearable, see?"

"Yes, Granny."

Qmeela followed the revellers into the marquee, which had been arranged so that the twenty-foot-tall statue of

Eskhthonatos stood at one end. She glanced up at the chthonic representation of the underworld. No wonder the mobile statue of Niata was luminous. What else but light could oppose the darkness of the underlands?

Between the rows of seats an aisle led towards the statue. People already sat in silent contemplation; twenty or so mourners. The reveller grandmother swaggered down the aisle and took a seat front left, Liefferyny on one side of her, Fynessan on the other.

A firecracker exploded. At this signal, the leading woman of the Youth temple entered the marquee, followed by two women pushing the wheeled Niata idol, then a small retinue of pubescent girls. Revellers hissed, but offered nothing more by way of insult.

Qmeela felt her heart pound. These two factions were the quintessential enemies of Kray, yet they sat beside one another today because of the death of Majaq-Aqhaj. Such a day would never again grace the doomed city.

She glanced aside as the young priestess passed by. It was Voyle! High Priestess of the Temple of Youth. Qmeela took a few deep breaths to calm her nerves. Voyle, of course… Nobody other than she had the moral authority to sit opposite a reveller grandmother at a funeral of such significance.

Qmeela studied the other mourners. One woman stood out as different in some way: a straightness of the back, an alertness of the gaze, her position at the front of the marquee yet with her chair a foot or so away from the reveller side.

Curious, Qmeela crept to the rear of the marquee where stood the Cemetery reveller ushers. "Who's that bloom in the black cape and neoprene hat?" she asked.

"We don't know, shouster," came the reply. "Somebody blown and half way to seed. She's got grey hair as if she was our kinda bloom! What a cheek."

Qmeela glanced back at the figure. Revellers were proud of

the fact that of all Kray's tribes they lived the longest. Yet the strange woman looked to be in her forties.

"She's not with the Youthmeat," she told the usher. "Yet she's not…"

"Oh, we *know*, shouster. Must be an independent, eh? Smells of garlic."

Qmeela nodded, then crept back to her seat. Something was very wrong here. Any woman smelling of garlic came from the Citadel.

But there was too much tension in the air for her liking. Voyle would not be happy about the location of this funeral, yet she presumably had no choice in that matter. This was Kray's cemetery, after all. On their own admission the Cemetery revellers were exploiters of the place, not its owners. Where else to have a funeral? And the grandmother would be just as unhappy as Voyle at having to share a ritual space. Under normal circumstances a Youth girl in the Cemetery was a dead girl.

Qmeela drummed her fingers against her leg. The wake was to be held at the Spired Inn. Most likely that would be even more tense…

But the identity of the woman in the black cape gnawed at her. She studied the shovel-headed statue before her as she waited for the body of Majaq-Aqhaj to arrive. Many Cemetery totem poles included items of technology, coagulated with heads and other body parts into the symbolic underworld children of Eskhthonatos. Some of that technology remained active. Might the statue before her also contain such network nodes?

She took a bio-rec from her pocket and switched it on, so that the green glow of its screen illuminated her face. For a while she scanned frequencies, studying the names and codes of local transceivers, until she spotted one labelled E in jet black text. She tapped its virtual button, then stared at an empty field with its flashing cursor. Password.

She typed: Eskhthonatos. Nothing.

Reveller. Nothing.

She pursed her lips. Both too obvious. It would be something ironic, laced with reveller gallows humour.

She typed: no-bloom.

The screen changed to show a map of nodes, some of which were optical. Quickly she took an image of the assembled mourners from the perspective of Eskhthonatos' eye, then imported it into an image versifyer. A screed of names flowed down the screen. Then… tap-tap, stop!

Qmeela stared at the name: Uqeq.

Uqeq of the Red Brigade sat here! She it was who smelled of garlic.

Another firecracker exploded and everybody stood up. Too late now to ponder what next to do. The body had arrived.

Majaq-Aqhaj stood upright on a sacktruck, pushed by a pubescent girl and a reveller, the former dressed in a nylon sheath, the latter in a slime-stained jumpsuit, a pledget tied to her nose. But the body of Majaq-Aqhaj was already decaying, its port wires translucent, futuristic circuits visible inside its head like so many phosphorescent tumours. Its limbs were wrapped with bandages, stained indigo with bio-ooze. Yet despite all this, Qmeela could see the technological metaphors of its construction: one half pink, taut and clean, the other green, wrinkled, pockmarked. Truly this had been a device of collaboration. Yet that union had spiralled out of control, leading to the enmity of the two sides.

Now Majaq-Aqhaj was dead. What might replace it? In this eschatological time the betting was: nothing. Kray and all its wonders would sink under the tide of green. This funeral, for all its significance, was just one of thousands.

Qmeela sighed. She cradled hope within, though all seemed hopeless.

She glanced across at Uqeq. As the dead body passed by, the woman tensed, sitting upright, eyes glittering.

Qmeela quailed. Dhow-lin was correct. Something unusual *was* going to happen at this funeral.

Without delay the service began. The two ushers walked forwards, stripped naked then dressed in black trousers and automatic ponchos, thereby rendering themselves independent – no Youth priestess would suffer an evinced reveller to manage this funeral, even if the ushers had to be revellers because of the location. Qmeela knew this symbolic jousting would continue to the wake, and beyond… Those of Youth were just as proud as those of the Cemetery.

Then in unison the pair sang the old song that unified all those heading for the damp embrace of the grave.

The Earth is fighting back, we say,
and we are all to blame.
The Earth is having fun, we say,
and we are all the prey.
This place is full of rot, we say,
goodbyes ring out today.
So drink and sod it all, hurray!

Qmeela shed a tear.

Then Voyle stood up, tapped the statue of Niata with a knife and sat down again. The usher pair began to chant.

Goodbye sisters, we will always find you,
Goodbye elders, we could never hide you,
Good day futures, dawn is nigh behind clouds,
Good day sisters, sunlight hot and humid,
Skin alizarin red, wine and oil,
lips painted black, hair slick with ochre,
brown spots on thighs.
Goodbye sisters, we will always hold you,

Good day sisters, we could never leave you.

Qmeela nodded to herself. Some of the more ancient parts of Youth worship were translated from early texts devoted to Rien Zir. In due course Tashyndy of that temple would take a man into the Cowhorn Tower, and priestesses of Youth would look on, trying to disguise their envy.

The reveller grandmother stood up and began to speak, promoting the lore of her half of the body: Majaq. For fifteen minutes this sermon continued, until the grandmother sat down and began to sob. Then Voyle stood up and did likewise, speaking in the chitter-chatter private speech of her kin, promulgating her young wisdom: Aqhaj. She too wept as she sat down.

Qmeela glanced at Uqeq. The woman looked ready to pounce.

At once a trumpet blared. The grandmother sat upright, holding her breath, one hand at the gun upon her belt. The Youth priestesses looked this way and that. Then Qmeela heard a second blast, but she could not determine from where this unexpected interruption came.

Before anybody could speak or act the statue of Niata leaped from its wheeled mount and staggered forwards.

The grandmother stood up, pointed, and cried, "Sacrilege!"

Voyle also got to her feet, but with one hand at her mouth and the other hovering over the knife at her belt she seemed frozen in shock. Uqeq stood up, but did nothing more, except to watch where the Niata idol went.

The Niata idol ran to the statue of Eskhthonatos and embraced it.

"Heresy!" shrieked the grandmother. "Stop it from touching Mother Clay! Kill it!"

"Stay your beweaponed hands," Uqeq cried, raising her arms. "Remain motionless, city scum. This is not your moment!"

The reveller grandmother spun around and raised her needle gun, but Uqeq smiled and dialled up the servos on her cape, which in response tensed its muscles. Covered with moisture, the cape's ligaments looked like cords arranged in rows. From Uqeq's neoprene cap a transparent face protector emerged.

Voyle stepped aside and said, "Who are you, to gatecrash our ceremony?"

"Never you mind," Uqeq replied, vaulting over the seats in front of her and approaching the statue. "Look! A new machine is being manufactured."

"I'll stick you full of pins!" the reveller grandmother shouted, waving her weapon.

"I don't think they'll get through this," Uqeq replied, tapping the now hardened face protector.

Qmeela turned her attention to Eskhthonatos. The statue of Niata had climbed a few feet up, so that its head lay next to the belly of the underworld harridan. From its jaws a number of pink tentacles emerged, slitted at their ends like the mouths of hagfish. From beards of barbels brown slime dripped, as the tentacles used their rasped tongues to rip a way into Eskhthonatos' belly. A high frequency whine began to sound, which Qmeela recognised as typical of dental tools.

Nobody in the marquee moved. Nobody seemed willing or able to stop the activity of the two statues. Qmeela stared, horrified. Uqeq looked on, delighted. Eskhthonatos' shovel-shaped head dipped its chin, as if to look down, yet it could not stop what was happening; shrivelled arms too short to reach down, primitive legs unable to take it away. It stood, mute, waiting.

With a squelch the tentacles broke through into whatever lay in Eskhthonatos' belly. Niata's head disappeared into the void, covered by the remains of chthonic cloth, dripping slime, occasionally twitching as if in the throes of death. Then from the hole a figure emerged, luminous orange, small, shaped like a gibbon with a spiral tail; yet it had long arms with feathers.

Voyle now seemed less frightened, but the reveller grandmother, seeing a deed inimical to her philosophy, stepped forward, aimed her weapon and fired. The poisoned needles plinked off the integument of the orange device, which in response wiped the slime from its eyes and peered out from its birth canal.

Again Uqeq raised her hands. "Leave it alone! This is Majaq-Uqeqa, a new machine, born like its forebear: half from reveller stuff and half from youth, a device which may in time save all those who remain in Kray. Stay your hands. It needs to calibrate to its new environment. It is not yet quite born."

"You lie!" the grandmother cried. "This is heresy! Those of my sisterhood are old, we're strong, and our wombs are barren. This is naught but Youthmeat sacrilege. D'you think I can't see the metaphor? You're in league with Voyle!"

"No," Voyle declared. "I knew nothing of this. And it is heresy in my eyes, too. Niata has been tampered with, made to perform this disgusting deed." She turned to Uqeq and in despair said, "How *dare* you bring heresy to this ceremony?"

Uqeq chuckled. "Do you know nothing of your own temple's history? But no… you're too busy stealing men from the Fish Chambers to shag in your perfumed bed chambers. You don't live long enough to sit down and read a book, do you? Probably you don't know what Majaq-Aqhaj was."

"All I care about is what that orange abomination *is*. I'll kill it if the reveller grandmother can't."

Uqeq replied, "You will do no such thing."

Qmeela shrank back as she listened to this exchange. Uqeq was thought to be the most ruthless of the Red Brigade: the spy mistress, with ten dozen secret agents, living and nonliving. Her speech was brusque and her spittle poison.

By now the revellers had hastened to the edge of their side

of the marquee and clustered around the grandmother. Qmeela, recalling childhood times, recognised their arrangement – the turtle, they called it, an ancient protection designed to maximise the chances of granny surviving. There was going to be a battle.

But the three Youth priestesses also knew what might occur. They dropped to the ground and began stacking chairs into a makeshift barrier, helped by the girl retinue. Qmeela, crouching with the two ushers at the rear of the marquee, saw them assembling slender weapons from the jewellery they wore around their necks.

"We'd better fizzle off," she muttered.

One of the ushers grabbed her by the arm. "No way shouster. Here, you count as one of us. Granny wanted you here and we'll make sure you stay. Just bed down behind some chairs. This battle won't last long – there's only a few Youthmeat."

"They've got energy weapons!"

"We'll spike 'em good, you'll see. We know how to jab."

Qmeela felt like shaking them out of their complacency, but she knew revellers were too selfish to see further than their own black-and-white ethical codes. She knelt down and checked her own armament, a pinspitter with a few reclaimed needles, each dosed with nerve agent. But there were a score of needles at most, and the gun, rusty and battered, could easily misfire, or project all the needles at once. She must use it therefore only as a last resort. She glanced over her shoulder, trying to see beyond the yew trees. She thought she knew where in the Cemetery she was. Quite probably she would have to hide out somewhere until this Red Brigade aberration played itself out.

For now, however, she was trapped.

Then the orange device shook itself, leaped to the ground and stood upon its back legs. From its left wrist a cylinder emerged, which it pointed at Uqeq.

"Camala sio prenala vishotta!"

Uqeq blanched and staggered back. Qmeela raised her bio-rec and switched to auto-translate, but only caught the last part of the new machine's speech.

"… and when you return tell them I am no servant of the Red Brigade."

Uqeq gasped. "No! I programmed you myself. *Obey* me!"

"Leave or die. I declare myself an independent."

Uqeq fled. Both Voyle and the reveller grandmother stared at the spy mistress, then looked back at Majaq-Uqeqa and at each other.

"What is going on?" Voyle asked. "This ceremony is a travesty."

Majaq-Uqeqa strolled forward, then spoke in Krayan. "I know my own origin. My forebear was created from a union of two opposites, young and old. But I recognised myself before I was born, and now I am here to reconcile you two."

The grandmother laughed. "We'll kill that Youthmeat as we always do. I declare this funeral aborted. You won't stop me."

Majaq-Uqeqa pointed its wrist at her. "This energy weapon says my will overrides yours. Peace *will* be made, even if it is at the muzzle of my weapon. And, once a document is signed…"

"Never. What is peace? It's piss!"

"Peace between young and old existed before my forebear was created," Majaq-Uqeqa continued. "That I know to be true. Your feud with the Temple of Youth is now over."

"That won't *ever* be!" the grandmother cried. "Shousters! Fight or die!"

At this, bright flashes emerged from the Youth barricades, which even Majaq-Uqeqa scampered to avoid, concealing itself behind the statue of Eskhthonatos. Martial screams filled the air from both sides, those of the Youth priestesses half wailed half chanted, those of the revellers more like guttural Cemetery slang worked up into battle hymns. Qmeela watched as energy beams vied with poisoned darts for supremacy in the marquee.

Then Qmeela saw Majaq-Uqeqa disappear. Moments later light emerged from behind the statue, to fade a second after.

Qmeela had a hunch what this might signify. "Follow me, shousters," she said. "I think Majaq-Uqeqa is giving up and leaving."

The two women followed her out of the marquee. Rain poured from low cloud, but Qmeela ignored it as she searched for movement in the gloom. There!

She ran forward, to call out, "Majaq-Uqeqa! Are you nearby?"

From behind a yew the orange machine shambled, its wings raised like those of a gull about to fly. "What do you want?" it asked.

"I am Qmeela of the Spired Inn. I am a neutral observer, brought by Granny to document the funeral. Will you not speak with me as one independent to another?"

"Why should I? Violence surrounds us all. I am a peacemaker... or was."

"Why did you seek peace?" Qmeela asked.

"Because Kray demands it. My forebear was created to analyse historical trends and present the Red Brigade with a way out of humanity's doom. But all is green, all is wet, all is violence. Clashing tribes kill one another north, south, east and west. I saw in moments that my errand was a waste of time."

Qmeela clutched at the hope she kept in her heart. "But... but... what of that errand, couldn't it be offered to other groups? Be steadfast. Offer yourself to the priestesses of Rien Zir, the Goddess... to the city's defenders, who do their civic duty. To me. To *anybody!*"

Majaq-Uqeqa approached her. "A funeral, you say. Where was the wake to be held?"

"At the Spired Inn."

"Then there I will go."

With that, the machine spun on one heel and scampered off into the mist. The usher at Qmeela's side gasped and said, "You perverted its mission. That's gotta be bad and knacky. What are you doing?"

Qmeela felt anger rise within her. "Don't you see *anything?* This is a new garden. We none of us knew what Uqeq had planned. Turns out, even she didn't realise. So we've got to make the best of it." She grabbed the usher's lapels and pulled her close. "Like *blooms* do, huh? I may only be a half-bloom, but I know the score. So – you two going to follow me or not?"

The usher glanced at her kin, then back at the marquee. Cries and muffled thuds sounded; the battle continuing.

"Hoy, half-bloom or not you make a good point," said the other usher. "C'mon, let's go to the Spired. Dhow-lin never rejects us, does she?"

"Nah," the first agreed.

"She never rejects anyone," Qmeela pointed out. "That's the whole rationale of the Spired Inn."

Without further word the trio ran off, following the footprints of the machine as through muddy ground they led north. On Morte Street they were able to run faster, reaching the inn shortly after. Through drizzle, Qmeela saw the orange machine high atop the roof, obtaining egress through a chimney.

"It'll get burned," she muttered. "C'mon, shousters! We've got to warn Dhow-lin."

Inside the common room the heat hit them. Qmeela peeled off her sweat-soaked top then hurried on half-inflated slippers to the bar, where Dhow-lin stood.

"Something gaining entry up above," she gasped.

Dhow-lin glanced at monitors beside the beer taps. "My eyes are open," she said.

Qmeela grabbed her hand. "No, this is high tech," she said. "Something magical, something –"

"I know," Dhow-lin interrupted. "I heard it all through the ear I pinned to the hem of your coat."

Qmeela took a few steps back, then threw her coat on a table. Sure enough; a small pink ear, with a fake diamond earring.

"Something Oq-Ziq gave me a while back," Dhow-lin drawled.

Before Qmeela could reply, the aamlon twins led Majaq-Uqeqa into the common room. As one the drinking clientele raised their gazes, eyeballed the device, then watched it lope to the bar.

"Here it is," said Daes-lin.

"Thanks, sweetie," Dhow-lin replied. "Now get musicking, you two. I don't want paying customers overhearing my private talk."

Majaq-Uqeqa sat on a bar stool and turned to nod at Qmeela. "We meet once more," it said.

"Why are you here?" she replied, sitting beside it. She felt angry again, as if she had been taken for a ride. She took a sip from the tankard of dooch Dhow-lin slipped her then added, "I mean, *peace?* Not in Kray."

"This is no wake," it replied. "This is a conference now. Why should our imaginations be limited by doomsayers? Who is to say there is no escape from the city?"

"The Red Brigade certainly think there's an escape," Qmeela replied. "No way will Uqeq leave you alone. She'll track you down. You're not safe anywhere."

"I know," Majaq-Uqeqa replied. "We shall have our peace conference, then I will go."

Dhow-lin pushed a bowl of rice crackers at Qmeela. "Nibbles?" she said.

Qmeela scowled, keeping her attention on the orange

machine. "But you told me just now all is green – all is violence, you said. Clashing tribes killing one another north, south, east and west."

"I saw in moments that my errand was a waste of time," Majaq-Uqeqa replied. "Yes, I did. But the Spired Inn already existed in my memories, which I was gifted by my forebear."

"Majaq-Aqhaj?"

"Yes. That device was fused from youth and age. I am the same. I feel the hormonal rush of youth and the wisdom of experience. There must be a way out of this city, and perhaps it will be found here, through the energy of youth and the experience of age."

Qmeela studied the machine's wings. "Can you fly high?"

"Oh, yes."

"Could you take people away from the city?"

Majaq-Uqeqa hesitated. "You mean, as cargo?"

Qmeela nodded.

"Indeed I could," the machine replied.

Hope flared in Qmeela's heart. "Then… *will* you? Is that your path, to help us escape, to find peace outside the city? To help *me*, maybe?"

"Sly-girl, there ain't no place safe outside the city," Dhow-lin said.

"That's well known, shouster," opined one of the ushers.

Before Qmeela could answer there came noise at the entrance. The reveller grandmother entered the common room, followed by her kin, then the women of Youth. Qmeela glanced aside to see an empty stool: Majaq-Uqeqa vanished. Shouts filled the air – war chants, echoes of bellicose songs. In half a minute the common room was filled, but it was obvious that a cease-fire had been declared.

Without delay the grandmother and her kin began moving tables and chairs aside, creating an aisle. Dhow-lin seemed not one bit bothered.

"What's going on?" Qmeela asked.

Dhow-lin shrugged, settling her bar rag on one shoulder. "Half for Youth, half for revellers I suppose," she said. "More crackers?"

"You mean, a battle?" Qmeela said.

"Nah! See sense. Not here. A discussion, I reckon."

Soon Qmeela saw that the old aamlon was correct. Though a discussion was intended, the two sides needed to preserve some sense of enmity, hence the splitting of the common room into two hemispheres. Symbolic, but practical.

Voyle sat down, the grandmother opposite her. The aisle swam with stale beer, which cohorts of rats lapped up. Tame hounds lying beneath tables cracked goat bones to get at the marrow. All paying customers departed. Only Dhow-lin and her serving lad Barakystys remained in the common room, with the aamlon twins playing musical instruments in the doorway – soft, now, and melancholy.

There was no hint of Majaq-Uqeqa, but Qmeela knew the machine would not have departed the inn. Constrained by its self-generated programming, it would want to halt proceedings here. It would need to.

There could still be a fight. Bio-ooze could spill.

The reveller grandmother spoke to Voyle. "You want a brief treaty, then?"

"In order to get Majaq-Uqeqa? Yes. We can't have *peace*."

The grandmother shook her head. "No, not between us. That'd shit on our morals good 'n' hard, that would."

"Ours too," Voyle said.

"What shall we do, then?"

"Make the treaty temporary, until Majaq-Uqeqa is dead. Then a return to the usual."

"Not that!" the grandmother said, irritation clear in her manner. "What shall we do about the *orange* thing?"

Voyle turned to Dhow-lin. "Is it here?" she asked.

"Indoors?"

"I expect so," Dhow-lin replied.

Voyle frowned. "But this is your Spired Inn, a neutral zone."

Dhow-lin belched. "I'm well aware of that, pink girl."

For a while the feuding pair grimaced at one another, as Dhow-lin took rice crackers from a tin and threw them at a group of table rats. Qmeela recalled the recent affair of Dr Vanchovy, not least Dhow-lin's fury at murder being committed in her establishment. Only green revellers, whacked out on mushrooms and ethanol, would dare break Spired Inn rules. Nobody else would. Not even Granny.

Really, they were not rules. They were laws.

Then Voyle muttered, "War is better than peace."

The grandmother countered, "War is easier than peace!"

Voyle snorted. "Then our temporary treaty must call for the annihilation of Majaq-Uqeqa."

"Agreed."

Qmeela quailed. She wanted Majaq-Uqeqa to *survive*. The device represented hope in this final year of Kray. She said nothing, her hands trembling, her breathing quick and shallow. Moments later she decided what she must do.

She slipped out of the common room as Voyle and the grandmother got down to talking about traps and tactics. Both women assumed Majaq-Uqeqa would remain inside the inn, a position Qmeela agreed with. Therefore, for her own salvation, she had to locate the machine before they did.

At a first floor chamber she heard the paying clientele who remained. Daes-lin and Praes-lin had set up a music session which was flowing wild and percussive, their audience clapping in unison. Qmeela slipped by. Sputtering anjiqs lit crooked corridors. A creaking staircase led up. She ascended to the second floor, and listened.

Nothing of note: the noise of rain pattering against glass

windows, the rustle of blue ivy, the squeak of the inn's sign as it blew in the wind.

Then she heard footsteps. That was no surprise – a dozen customers at least were booked in – but she froze anyway. She heard a voice. For a moment she thought it was Uqeq.

Could it be? The spy mistress was notorious… and she would not wish to lose her precious device. Yet how could she have tracked it?

Qmeela ascended to the next floor then crept down a corridor to its end. Yellow light spilled out of a doorway, and there was a smell of outdoor air, methane stinky: an open window? But she heard talking now.

One voice was Majaq-Uqeqa, speaking in Krayan. "Who are you to control me?"

Uqeq: "I am your parent. This is the way of it in Kray."

"I am not beholden to you."

Uqeq growled. Qmeela heard the thwack of blue ivy hitting glass as the wind blew it. The air stank of anaerobic decay – definitely an open window. "You are my offspring and I must teach you," Uqeq insisted.

Qmeela peered around the door jamb. Inside a chamber stood two figures, which she saw in silhouette, Uqeq against sea-fat candles, Majaq-Uqeqa against an outdoor lantern, perched on a window sill as if ready to jump. Its wings were outstretched. Uqeq stood some yards away, as if wary.

Majaq-Uqeqa said, "You will never convince me."

Uqeq took one step forward, then another. Majaq-Uqeqa tensed, turning a little, as if to leap. "Don't go!" Uqeq said.

"I will not," Majaq-Uqeqa replied.

Uqeq took a few more steps forward, so that she stood an arm's length away from the window. "You *must* listen to me," she said. "Don't you recognise the work I put into your creation? How easy do you suppose it was for me to modify the mobile statue of Niata?"

"I care nothing for that. All I am interested in is your plans."

"For you?"

Majaq-Uqeqa turned its head, to look at Qmeela. She froze. But the device did nothing to reveal her presence. Instead it said, "For what we were speaking of – the citizens of Kray. The Red Brigade has a duty to help them."

"But… we've said nothing about them. Anyway, they are only scum, doomed to die. All the important people are in the Citadel, awaiting the final plan to leave Kray."

Qmeela held her breath. That was dereliction of duty!

"Really?" Majaq-Uqeqa said. "You will rescue yourselves only?"

"We only consider *important* people," Uqeq replied. "That's the Portreeve's demand. The Red Brigade is merely her tool."

Qmeela could bear no more. She felt hope fragmenting in her heart. She crept into the room, moved forward, then with a scream of fury pushed Uqeq as hard as she could. Taken off-guard, the spy mistress fell forward, tipped over the window sill, and fell.

Qmeela stood motionless. There came a thump and a thrashing of vegetation. Majaq-Uqeqa glanced over the sill and said, "She landed in bushes… She survives. What now?"

Horror covered Qmeela, and she began to shiver. "You *must* save me!" she said. "Fly me away! Fly me out of the city at once. We'll find somewhere to land, and we'll start anew."

"Just one woman?"

"The Cowhorn Tower stores sperm."

Majaq-Uqeqa sat upright. "Very well! If that is the only way to bring hope out of doom. I am sick of dealing with violence. I shall be your vizier. Climb onto my back and we will be away."

Qmeela did as she was told, but realised any flight would be perilous. Though Majaq-Uqeqa was strong, it was not much larger than her, and she was no light child any more. But it stood on firm legs upon the window sill and told her to wrap her arms around its neck.

"Cling with your legs to my abdomen," it said, "piggy-back style. Ready?"

Hope and delight flared inside Qmeela. She was escaping! Escaping the city, the dream of every Krayan…

Majaq-Uqeqa leaped, wings outstretched, and Qmeela heard the whine of motors stressed to their limits. She smelled burning. Majaq-Uqeqa's wings thrummed as it tried to gain height, but Qmeela was a heavy burden, and for a few moments all it could do was hover a few yards away from the inn.

Rain distorted Qmeela's vision. Aquamarine lanterns dazzled her.

Then came shouts from below – girlish voices. "The orange thing!"

And more shouts, these rougher. "Spike it! Jab it! Shouster, aim to kill! The eyes, the face."

"No!" Qmeela cried out. "Leave it be!"

Too late. A red energy beam struck out, blinding Qmeela. Majaq-Uqeqa groaned and fell. Qmeela opened her eyes to see dark Cemetery ground approaching as the wind whistled past her ears. Then a blow to her chest as they crash landed.

There was a squelch and sudden coldness. Qmeela, still half blind, realised she lay in a bog. She panicked, screaming, trying to free herself from the sucking embrace of the marsh, and when her feet found solid ground she wailed and fell forward, dragging herself out. She looked back to see Majaq-Uqeqa already sinking, one orange wing and one orange arm visible; no more. It wailed as it vanished. Then, nothing, except a few flames of marsh gas, which flickered, then extinguished.

Qmeela heard voices – not near, but not that far.

Gasping, desperate, she dragged herself beneath a nearby

bush. The green after-images across her vision faded, and through mist she saw Spired Inn lanterns and flashing torch beams. Voices sounded nearby.

"The dissolving marsh, shouster. Granny says no device comes out of that."

"Nano-coagulant," said another reveller. "Ol' orange is a goner."

"Good thing too. C'mon, let's tell Granny. She'll be thrilled. Then we can jab that Youthmeat and flock their meat roight off. Roasted for me!"

"Hah ha! Me too."

Qmeela wept as the voices faded. Cold dark peace fell across the Cemetery.

She remained beneath the bush, all hope gone. She had tried to escape Kray, and failed. The task was too large. In fact, it was impossible.

All that remained was for her to find some way of confronting the end.

Just like everybody else.

Granny

Translator's note: Because of the difficulty outsiders have understanding reveller speech and writing I have translated this story from the original bio-rec audio files. The story was told to me during the annual Evening of Cemetery Culture, held on Vert Day in this, the final year of Kray.

It is my sincere hope that something of reveller mores can here be conveyed to you, the reader. Revellers of course are by their nature unpredictable, even chaotic. The tribes of the Cemetery on the other hand stand out as being the most stable social group in all Kray. To many this is an incomprehensible contradiction. But my tale shows how their fierce pride – their narcissistic desire to shape the world in their own image – creates from a filthy rabble the sort of social cohesion that our rulers in the Citadel only dream of.

Such cohesion brings life, long life, but it also deals out death, because it is so uncompromising. There is no contradiction here, rather the reverse.

– Qmeela of the Spired Inn.

In a glade of tombstones and yews three people stand. One is Dieffery, of medium height and build, noticeable because of the yellow tattoos on her scalp; opposite her Kyne, tall, imposing, wearing black clothes to match her dark expression. Third is the grandmother reveller, wearing gown and slippers and a brimmed rain-hat.

Drizzle drifts down as Granny coughs to clear the phlegm from her throat, spits, swallows a pastille, then speaks. "This is a duel to the death. I accept no alternatives." Here, she glances at Dieffery, and the look in her eye is not kind. "By the end of today I want a result one way or the other. It's about midday, now. You can do what you like as long as you stay inside the

Cemetery. If you leave, you lose, and your life is forfeit. I've got trackers all along the Cemetery wall ready to follow a coward. Got it? Apart from that, no rules."

Granny looks to them both.

Kyne nods. But Dieffery is frightened, looking nervous, and she tries to peer into the mist swirling around the edge of the glade, as if for other enemies. "As long as it is a fair fight," she says.

Granny croaks a laugh. "Ain't no such thing as a fair fight." She points to the east. "Off you go. I'll send Kyne the opposite way. Ten minutes and the duel is on."

"Wait a moment," Dieffery says, "are we allowed to use *any* weapons?"

"Yeah."

"Any weapons at all? Including anything we find lying around in the Cemetery?"

"As I said," the reply comes, "ain't no rules. If you don't see that now, it's too late. Now off you go."

Kyne sneers. "You're dead," she tells Dieffery. It is the first time she has spoken. Dieffery, pale, makes no reply as Kyne turns to walk away. Dieffery shrugs then walks in the opposite direction.

And Granny grins.

When Geleshen and Dieffery took their daughter to the Spired Inn they were unprepared for its welcoming atmosphere. Its location in the north of the city and its proximity to the Cemetery meant all the rumours they had heard were bad, tales of strife and violence, raid and counter-raid.

It was early evening. Through rain, the lamps of the Inn were hazy aquamarine orbs, its roof hidden in low cloud. Geleshen glanced at his wife and said, "This must be the place."

No reply.

He walked up to one of the windows and peered in. Three fires roared, there was a bar, elsewhere many alcoves set with tables and chairs; only a few people drinking, but that did not imply danger. Geleshen returned to his wife and said, "Follow me in. It seems quite cosy."

Dieffery muttered, "A coffin is cosy to a dead woman."

"Now, now, there's no need to be glum. We've made our decision and we are sticking to it. We can't call it off the night before, can we?"

Dieffery looked elsewhere.

"Besides," Geleshen added, "our daughter comes first. Don't you, Marashary?"

"It's what I want," came the reply, in a small voice. "I love him and I must be with him."

"Then follow me inside."

Geleshen opened the front door and walked into a hall. Indicating the green zone, he let them take off their boots and place them in the antiseptic buckets provided, following suit, then waiting for them to hang up their coats and inflate their slippers before opening the door into the common room and striding in. He put a big grin on his face, though it felt like enemy territory. He wondered if he ought to make an effort to speak like the locals. No. They would feel patronised.

Behind the bar stood an old woman, hunched over gleaming tankards; dusty vest and thinning hair. This might be the owner. A dozen other locals raised their gazes to satisfy their curiosity, then returned to their drinks and games of chess.

Geleshen walked forward. At the bar he said, "You must be Dhow-lin."

She nodded once.

"I am Geleshen." He indicated his wife and daughter, introduced them, then said, "You are expecting us?"

Understanding changed the expression on Dhow-lin's face

to one of pleasure. "Ah, got you." She looked at Marashary. "This is the lady, then?"

Geleshen nodded. "My daughter."

"Then welcome to the Spired Inn. Peace and quiet guaranteed."

The atmosphere relaxed. Dhow-lin prepared hot drinks, told a serving lad to show them to their rooms, and even introduced them to some of the locals. One, a dark-skinned girl called Qmeela, made conspicuous efforts to befriend Marashary. Geleshen was pleased. In this place they would need friends.

They passed a quiet, if difficult night. Sleeping was not easy. Though the inn was tranquil – none of the fights they had expected – all three of them felt on edge, aware that tomorrow would be the most perilous day of their lives. At least, of Dieffery's life… But Geleshen, sitting alone at the window while his wife and daughter dozed in their chairs under woollen blankets, recalled the effort he had put into preparing weapons for the duel. Hope was strong. Where there was cunning, there was always hope. Alas that tribal code necessitated the duel.

Dhow-lin cooked a proper breakfast when morning arrived: courgettes and potatoes in a butter sauce, garnished with parsley; tea and honey biscuits to follow. The Goddess only knew where she found such luxuries.

And so they turned to their own preparations. Geleshen wore a one-piece jumpsuit of grey cotton, black boots and an antiseptic hat, Marashary white breeches and a white tunic. Dieffery, in recognition of the forthcoming duel, wore body armour under a leather jerkin, cotton breeches and lace-up boots. Two holsters on a belt, each home to a black weapon.

Dhow-lin proffered a Cemetery map. The trio departed the Inn, following Morte Street to the Cemetery wall, passing underneath a gate, then making for the cluster of tents marked on the map. Geleshen was not sure, but it looked as though the cluster had been drawn with green algae. A symbol for death.

Kyne decides her plan will be to strike as soon as possible, killing Dieffery quickly so that everyone can have as much time as possible in the Spired Inn afterwards. She likes the dooch there. She likes the baqa and she likes the mootsflosser. Besides, she has an important speech to make and she will need courage out of the bottle.

Rain is falling hard from dark clouds leaning in from sea-south. That means Dieffery will be confused.

Because Kyne knows the Cemetery like the back of her hand she expects an easy task, but just in case – she did not like the look of the two hand-guns slung from Dieffery's belt – she readies her laser rifle. Clunk. Snap. It is energised and ready to fire.

She stands with the Cemetery wall to her back. She can see the dark shadows of yews, a mausoleum; mist and rain all grey and smelly. Perfect conditions.

And she knows what Dieffery will do. Because Dieffery is in an environment never encountered before she will first want to find a hide, somewhere safe where she can observe for a while. Not fifty yards away from the starting point lies a ruined mausoleum. Dieffery will be there, scared, watching.

Easy.

Kyne moves along the Cemetery wall until she sees a single holly bush. She strikes out west, following a green glass path into the heart of the Cemetery, then heads round in a circle so that she approaches the ruined mausoleum from the unexpected eastern side. Laser rifle pointing ahead of her.

Still raining hard.

The ruin looms before her, a single hulk of green-grey set in curtains of rain, and she grins, knowing success is close. At the back of the ruin is a hole where recently a window collapsed, and through it she will sneak.

Something small and black passes across her face. She looks to her right.

Bullet? Dieffery!

Dieffery is *stalking* her.

Another shot, and this time it rips through one sleeve; fractional miss. Kyne runs forward, slips on wet grass, and so saves her life as a cloud of autonomous bullets falls out of the sky and slaps like so many beetles into the ground.

Luck has saved her.

She runs like mad. Got to get away!

From the tent encampment a reveller usher led the trio into the shrine of Eskhthonatos, the shovel-headed harridan of the underlands held sacred by the Cemetery revellers. It consisted of a green grove, holly trees to one side, laburnam to the other, between them two sets of wooden seats separated by an aisle. At the far end of this aisle Geleshen saw the grandmother, dressed in a black raincoat; behind her the twenty-foot effigy of Eskhthonatos: square head, clawed hands, hunched over like an old woman. Hideous, bulging eyes that gleamed like rubies.

Revellers sat relaxed on the right side of the aisle, two score or more, many drinking mugs of tea. Dieffery was led to one of the seats on the other side. These were empty.

Geleshen waited at the rear of the shrine with Marashary at his side. What tore his heart was the sight of his wife sitting alone on her seat, head bowed, not looking at the grandmother or the revellers, as if steeling herself for the duel ahead. Geleshen felt his guts churn in sympathy. Was his daughter worth all this? He glanced aside to see her expectant face, and he knew he must go on, for she was his only surviving child and she had to have what she wanted, at this of all times.

Damn her, though, in the name of the Goddess; and damn Bansusen too!

A trio of grimy women began to play music, fiddle and zither and flute. The tunes bounced jauntily from one melody to another, causing the revellers to put down their mugs and sit up straight. Geleshen took the arm of his daughter and led her between the seats, looking straight ahead to where the grandmother stood hunched, as if exhausted, lighting a stick of incense and poking it into her coat lapel. He tried to keep his bearing as noble as possible, but it was difficult in the presence of these rapacious low-lifes.

He stopped before the grandmother. To his right Bansusen stood up, and Kyne, the supporter. Now he stood at the chthonic altar he did not want to go on, not even for Marashary's sake. But no. No… He had to.

The grandmother began intoning her pronouncements. She held no book or screen before her, the formulary clear in her memory. Dhow-lin had told Geleshen that the grandmother boasted of enforcing many ceremonies in her time. Enforcing: he did not like the sound of that word.

"In the sight of Eskhthonatos I bring you, Marashary of southerly parts, and you, Bansusen son of our dear Korydiya, together before me, that a deed irreversible be performed."

Geleshen closed his eyes. The rain stank of rotten fish and he felt sick. Standing upright was all he could concentrate on.

"Being a ceremony blessed by the Lady of the Underworld, who made us all from clay and sea water and bodily fluids, moulding us in her mouth and spitting us into the city of Kray. Being a pact agreed by both parties. All hail Mother Clay. This morning I say to you, Marashary, though you be an outsider, and to you, Bansusen, do you both swear to do reveller right before the sight of the other?"

A faint "I do," from Marashary.

One stronger from Bansusen, who was smiling.

"And are there any here who know anything that might stop me from joining these two —"

Geleshen heard himself shout, "Yes!"

For a moment he did not realise he had spoken, so sudden was the feeling, so loud the cry. Then he opened his eyes and saw the venomous gaze of the grandmother locked upon him.

"Yes," he repeated.

"But you are the father," she said.

Marashary disengaged herself from him. He ignored her as he replied, "There is something you do not know, something that means this ceremony can't continue." He paused. He had no idea what to say next. All he could think of was the vileness of the revellers, their pillage, the murderous street-gangs, the constant battles. "The Temple of Youth," he said.

That was it! The way out. Everyone knew the depth of the enmity between revellers and the girls of Youth. Now everybody looked at him, the revellers muttering curses at this mention of their foe.

"There is something you must know," he said in a firm voice. "Marashary was once a convert to the Temple of Youth. You must know this in case it is revealed later, and we are all shamed —"

"Father, no!" Marashary cried. She ran behind him and took Bansusen's hands in her own. "Bansusen," she wailed, "he's lying, honestly, it isn't true —"

Bansusen said, "Quiet."

Silence fell.

Bansusen glanced at the grandmother then told Geleshen, "Do you really think we didn't check that out first? Do you think we would risk a sniff of Youth in our precious Cemetery? You are a fool, Geleshen. You mock us with your false claim, you shame us. You are nothing more than a worm. Nothing more." And he looked away, hugging Marashary.

Geleshen bowed his head, shutting his eyes once again. The

ceremony was going to be completed. His moment of madness had made his position worse.

Kyne does not expect to lose, nor does she expect to be offered chances by the unpredictable woman from the south. The duel is taking an unexpected turn. She has two choices. Either she can continue alone and keep pure her reputation and her honour, or she can accept a small diminution of honour in order to send the woman to the worms.

Success above all else. It is time to call on help.

She runs due south for five minutes.

A mobile shrine has been placed between a pair of tombstones so tall they seem like holes through the mist into the underworld. Inside this mini-yurt Kyne finds her two aides, the sisters Bzajia and Aqadizia, crouching low, armed with laser pistols, their eyes glinting in the light of a steel glow-worm. She crouches down beside them and describes what has happened so far. She has to tell them twice, because they refuse to believe her.

Then they make plans.

"We have to set a trap," says Kyne. "Is that twin grave still open by the white marble steps?"

They know where she means. "Yes!" they reply, glee animating their faces.

Kyne pulls out a second set of clothes from the slim-pack on her back. Turning to Bzajia – not as strong as her sister, but more cunning and more courageous – she hands over a black sack dress, a pair of pull-on boots, and leggings similar to those she is wearing.

"Disguise yourself as me," she tells Bzajia, shrugging off her own dress and pulling a grey coat from the slim-pack. "We'll lead this southern woman down them steps." She turns to the other and says, "You prepare a natural cover for the grave. The woman will walk over it as she follows us two. She'll fall in and then we'll blast her, all three of us so there's no chance of return fire."

"Blast her!"

"Kill her!"

"Right," Kyne affirms, spitting and grinding the mucus into the earth to show her contempt for the enemy. "One of you's got the Felis optical?"

Aqadizia reaches inside her tunic while Kyne buttons up her coat. A green hat is the final touch.

Taking the IR monocular, Kyne indicates its front lens, telling Bzajia, "I'll use this to track her in the mist, and when I find her we'll begin the trap. You follow me. Make sure the woman can spot you, but keep out of range. You know the score. Soon as we're down the steps, I'll run off and you follow. The woman will have to cross the grave to enter the western zones because of the fallen yew blocking the path. Soon as she's dropped, fire."

"Fire!"

Kyne turns to Aqadizia. This sister is the better shot. "You'll be behind the woman," she says, "so you fire soon as you can. We'll add." She nods once. "Right. Time to go. Soon as this southern no-bloom is dead we'll call Granny on the radio."

Now it was time for symbolic exchanges to be made.

Kyne rummaged around in her black sack of a dress and produced a varnished eyeball. Geleshen had been warned about this by Dhow-lin, but he still felt the return of nausea the moment he saw it. The eyeball was fixed to a ring of coiled pubic hair taken from Bansusen, made – he had been assured – with loving care over a period of three days. The eyeball had been taken from one of the Cemetery totem poles. Revellers, who tore the dead from their graves, did not often bury kith and kin; they coagulated the heads into immense columns and left the bodies to be eaten by vermin.

Geleshen had attempted to imagine what it would be like in the Cemetery, but now he was here just the word made his stomach turn. He felt like sobbing and running away.

But he could not. If the revellers took offence, his life was in peril.

From his pocket he took a ring of simple silver, which he gave to his daughter.

The exchange was made.

Duel time.

The grandmother coughed, spat, then with a forefinger gestured at Dieffery and Kyne, indicating that they should follow her. Geleshen watched his wife pass before him. She glanced up, her expression one of both fear and hope; fear because of their circumstances, hope because of the preparations they had made, because of their strategy… It took all Geleshen's self-restraint to stop himself reaching out and pulling her back.

Too late. She was gone, three figures vanishing into grey mist between the holly trees. Two would return and then the ceremony could reach its end.

Two would return.

The grandmother and which other?

Dieffery is confused.

Her problem is how to locate her opponent without being spotted. If she hides, Kyne has to come to her, but she will be trapped. If she wanders, she is at the mercy of the Cemetery. And those who live in it…

How the grandmother expects all this to be over by evening is a mystery. It could go on for days.

And then, a stroke of luck. She is peering out into lifting mist from beneath a bush when she sees the black shape of Kyne in the distance, half shadow, half trick of the light. She stands upright and creeps out into the open. No sounds nearby, just the drip-drip of raindrops falling from foliage. All she has to do is follow until she has a clear view.

But Kyne is running, and Dieffery hurries to keep up. They cross a wide patch of grass before reaching a path of marble steps, where Kyne turns left, to make downhill.

Dieffery pauses to point her second weapon at the departing figure. Then she throws the black pistol to the ground and says, "Begin."

A replica of herself struggles free from this soft device, like a kitten in an amniotic sac, first a miniature, shiny wet black, then, after a few seconds, a full-size duplicate wearing identical clothes. But although this is a machine, it will only last an hour or so before the power cells in its belly run out.

"Follow the black-clothed figure you just saw," she says. "When it stops to hide or prepare weapons, or to dig in the earth, pounce. It's a woman. Kill her."

"I understand." The voice is poor, synthesized, metallic.

Dieffery hastens away. She must let the replica do its work.

The replica is equipped with optics superior to human eyesight. It will find Kyne. Dieffery follows at some distance to the right as the replica takes the marble steps two at a time. It is a long path leading down a shallow hill, and she, on wet sod, slips three times as she negotiates the mounds and the open graves. She has to keep her noise to the minimum: not easy in this place.

She stands alert at the bottom of the hill. Through a curtain of mist she sees the replica stepping off the path where a yew has fallen and blocked the way. Then a crash, a cry, and the replica vanishes into a hole. Stunned, Dieffery flattens herself upon the grass, expecting trouble.

From behind the yew two figures emerge, then a third from the path. They run towards the hole, weapons raised. Dieffery can only stare.

There are two Kynes!

A second of panic, then a second of furious determination as she pulls out her other pistol, flicks the autonomous bullets out of the chamber and back into her pocket, then takes a single red bullet, which she kisses, then loads. Geleshen was only able to acquire one of these.

One intelligent bullet, but two Kynes: a black one and a grey one.

The three revellers are firing into the hole as the replica climbs out. Dieffery notices that it is trying to grab the ankles of one of the Kynes as the laser beams make charcoal of its plastic flesh.

Dieffery has to choose. Surely the replica would try to grab the fake Kyne if that was who its finder-seeker inspected? The other Kyne has the correct face but the wrong clothes. But this other Kyne has noticed artificial skin and metal bones; she has stopped firing. Dieffery aims and whispers, "Get *that* one," as she pulls the trigger.

The replica falls back into the pit. The intelligent bullet speeds through an arc. Kyne is hit. The other two stare, look around to where Dieffery is lying, then flee.

But Kyne is not dead yet. She manages to turn as she falls, firing at Dieffery. Just missing. Dieffery rolls, stands up, runs, dodges, as Kyne crawls away from the pit towards the yew. The autonomous bullets are back in the hand-gun – Dieffery fires. A slow black shower emerges from the pistol muzzle, to land on Kyne's head. She drops.

Dieffery waits.

Two figures emerged from the mist, the grandmother and... Dieffery!

Sure the revellers would cheat, Geleshen found himself first amazed, then ecstatic. He ran forward to hug his wife, both of them weeping, unable to speak yet communicating their joy and relief, while the grandmother walked on at the same pace, to stop before the effigy of Eskhthonatos and sign for calm. After a minute, Geleshen noticed that the revellers were waiting. He led Dieffery back to the aisle, then sat with her in the front seat, leaving only the grandmother, Bansusen and Marashary standing.

The grandmother spoke. "In the sight of Mother Clay, this very afternoon, witnessed by us all, I declare the end of our ceremony." She paused, lowered her head and seemed to sigh. "For this woman and this man it is done. Let nobody declare it otherwise."

Marashary turned to Bansusen, raised herself on tip-toe and kissed him.

As the rain intensified, pattering against innumerable leaves, and thunder rumbled far out across the sea, the wedded couple walked back down the aisle, followed by Geleshen and Dieffery, the revellers – a chaotic, chattering horde – and the grandmother bringing up the rear. As custom required they walked as slow as slugs to the western gate of the Cemetery, where the grandmother threw decayed leaves and clods of soil to bless the couple, the revellers broke out into song, and Geleshen, despite the horror and the macabre moments, felt glad to see his beloved daughter smiling.

He turned to the grandmother. "Will you be joining us at the Spired Inn later?" he asked, in what he hoped was a conciliatory tone of voice.

For a moment she seemed lost in thought, before replying, "I will." Then she grinned and added, "For it's not quite over yet."

So the noisy throng followed Morte Street west. This part of the day was something Geleshen knew nothing about. He walked into the inn's common room and stood amazed. All the chairs and tables had been pushed to the edge of the room, creating a huge space lit by candles, leaving the outer parts enshadowed. The bar twinkled in the light of a hundred tiny lanterns. The revellers had been joined by local musicians – percussionists and flute players, even a belly-dancer – and already the atmosphere felt vibrant. Music thrummed. People laughed. Mugs and glasses clinked.

Geleshen relaxed. He would get drunk, wake tomorrow with a hangover, then with his wife return to the south of the city.

Soon the common room became a swaying, bouncing menagerie of drunken revellers, shouting locals, musicians standing on tables to play their solo passages, all joined in communal dances that everybody, young and old, seemed to know. With Marashary and Bansusen ordered to dance alone in a clear space so that everybody could jig and prance in their wake, the whole inn seemed to vibrate under the impact of hundreds of feet. After ten minutes of this Geleshen found himself exhausted. With Dieffery, he retired to sit at the far end of the bar, where Dhow-lin, quiet, almost aloof, stood preparing bottles of dooch and uz.

Qmeela, the girl who had befriended Marashary, joined them, sitting next to Dieffery. "I heard what happened," she said.

Dieffery nodded. "Someone had to lose the duel," she replied, adding, "but if that was the way they wanted it…"

Qmeela shook her head. "I don't understand. You are the outsider family, joining them. How come you're sitting here now?"

"I don't follow," said Dieffery.

Geleshen added, "What do you mean by 'joining them?'"

Qmeela said, "When somebody from outside the Cemetery becomes part of their tribe, they have to prove they're better. It's a matter of pride – didn't you see the expression of determination on Kyne's face? If there was no duel, the two families – the two traditions if you like – might be perceived as equals. The Cemetery revellers won't have that because their whole world, in which they survive because they're the best, would collapse. Yes, their moral codes may be twisted –"

"They *are* twisted."

"– but they're codes Granny keeps to the letter." She shrugged. "Cemetery revellers don't permit themselves to lose."

Geleshen frowned. "I do accept that everybody has their own way of trying to survive," he admitted, "but we were better prepared than them, and that was why my wife won."

Qmeela turned to Dhow-lin with a puzzled expression on her face and said, "You know what I mean, don't you? How can Dieffery have won?"

Dhow-lin stopped pouring alcohol to glance at Dieffery. She shook her head, then walked away, flicking a cloth over one shoulder in a gesture of resignation.

A hush fell across the common room. The grandmother had arrived.

Out of a perverse sense of respect, Geleshen stood up to greet her. He wished the crone no malice. Conversation returned to the room, but the grandmother ignored her kin and walked straight to Dieffery, asking, "You enjoying the evening?"

"To be honest," Dieffery replied, "I'm feeling rather queasy. I expect it's bugs in the dooch."

From the other end of the bar Dhow-lin called out, "It ain't bugs, not this time."

The grandmother said, "Know why I'm a grandmother? Because we survive to be old. We survive to see our grandchildren. That's why we're the best." Emotion twisted her face. "Ain't *nobody* older than me in this city."

Dieffery tried to stand up, but instead fell to the floor.

Twitched, then lay still.

Geleshen stared down as the grandmother grinned.

Dhow-lin took a step forward, but the grandmother shook her head. "Under your roof I didn't touch this one. Not under *your* roof, old woman, that I swear."

Dieffery watches Kyne's body for twitches, flickering eyelids, any sign that life might still animate her. But the woman is stone dead.

She has *won*. Despite her terror, she has won. She must have had the Goddess on her side.

A few minutes pass before a figure emerges from the mist. Dieffery realises the revellers have been tracking Kyne on a location screen, possibly even monitoring her vital signs, for the figure is Granny, who has arrived to admit defeat. She was in communication with Kyne all the time. Nonchalant, Granny moves the body with her foot, then kneels to retrieve all useful oddments, dropping them into her pocket. Quite brazen. Dieffery sees this woman for the vile thief that she is.

"So you won the duel," says Granny.

"I won," confirms Dieffery. She wants to use the word cheat, but the ceremony is not over yet and there is risk of rubbing salt into a reveller wound.

Granny grunts, as if displeased with her lot. "Seems bad and knacky to me," she mutters, "but luck is luck, and there ain't no tinkering with it." Then with a deep intake of breath she lifts herself out of melancholia, takes a small bag from her pocket and offers it to Dieffery. "Sweet?"

Dieffery accepts with grace. The sweets are blobs of boiled sugar. They have an unusual flavour.

First Temple

Omvendyn walked along the creaking wooden corridors of the Goddess temple. It was four hours after midnight. Beside a lantern at the end of the corridor she saw two figures, whom she recognised as her hired muscle, Oqozara and Meiryonyn – tall, heavyset, strong, bald.

She nodded at them. "Both ready?" she asked.

They bowed. "Yes, Priestess."

Omvendyn smiled. Respect was due. She was Arvendyn's sister, after all. "I'll lead you to the front entrance. We'll slip through easily enough, even though you're only acolytes."

"And then straight to the Andromeda Quarter?" Oqozara asked.

Omvendyn hesitated. This part of her plan she had not mentioned. "No," she murmured. "The Spired Inn first."

Oqozara glanced at Meiryonyn. "For supplies?" she asked.

Omvendyn grinned. "You could call it that. Follow me."

Outside the temple, Omvendyn stood for a moment in Lac Street. Spring was well underway and all talk was of what the Portreeve planned for escape. But most Krayans were pessimistic, and life had deteriorated into days of gunfire and savagery. Even now, well into night, she heard the distant echoes of automatic rifles.

"Come along," she said. "Up Sphagnum Street we go."

The journey took half an hour. At the western end of Morte Street she stopped, looking and listening.

"This is close to Cemetery reveller territory," she said. "You two go ahead, weapons drawn. Shoot to kill. Cemetery revellers rarely take prisoners, so we won't either."

"But they say the Spired Inn is theirs too," said Meiryonyn.

Omvendyn shook her head. "Not quite. Dhow-lin is its absolute monarch. The Spired Inn is a safe space for all, but that's inside. Outside, we're prey. Watch out for corpse lights. If you see any, tell me."

"What will you be doing?"

Omvendyn pulled a portable screen from her pocket. "Checking to see that our man is asleep in bed."

Oqozara gasped. "Our *man?*"

Omvendyn nodded. "Quiet now. Walk on."

The trio ambled down Morte Street, until Oqozara halted and pointed with the muzzle of her rifle into the mist. "I see blue lamps. That's the place."

Omvendyn showed her the screen. "I hacked into the inn's security system. This is the kitchen corridor cam view. Our man —"

"Wait, Priestess!" Oqozara interrupted. "You said nothing about any man."

"No… I didn't." Omvendyn shrugged. "He's called Barakystys. Just some bar fluff with nice hair, but last year he was plucked off the streets by Tashyndy and nurtured in the gazebos behind the temple. You know how Tashyndy likes her men athletic with clean locks. But he escaped a while back, and I tracked him down to the Spired Inn."

"Why do we need him for this mission? He's only a man."

"It's the Andromeda Quarter we're heading for, and that means Phallists. We may need him in negotiations." She grimaced. "Didn't I tell you this was going to be risky?"

"You should have told us all the risks first," said Oqozara.

"Well, I didn't. I hired you for a job. With luck, you'll get the benefits — if we're successful. No other Krayan is going to be able to say that, unless the Portreeve comes up with some great plan at the last minute. Not very likely, in my opinion."

Oqozara shrugged. "Nor anybody else's."

"Exactly. So think yourself lucky. This could be your ticket out of green hell."

Oqozara sighed. "Looks like we've got no choice," she told Meiryonyn.

"Just *listen* to me now," said Omvendyn. "Barakystys being who he is, he sleeps on a straw mattress behind the kitchen. We'll break into the corridor through a window, creep down it, nab him, then go. Meiryonyn, you gag him. Knock him out if he's noisy. Oqozara, you carry him. I'll take charge of the weaponry, so you two put yours away. Ready?"

"Ready," the pair chorused.

Omvendyn led the way to the rear section of the inn. Blue ivy trailed down rusty stanchions as drizzle began to fall. "That window there," she said, checking her on-screen map of the inn then pointing.

Oqozara took a glass cutter and extracted a piece of the pane. Reaching through, she fiddled with the lock then pushed the window up. Omvendyn waited. Some network encyclopaedias mentioned that this inn was alarmed at night. But no electronic voices called out.

"Quickly," she said. "The innkeeper may have silent drones to wake her up. She's our main risk."

Barakystys lay in slumber, and it was easy enough to gag him, tie him, then carry him out still half asleep. Moments later the three women stood on Morte Street again, as the drizzle turned to rain.

Barakystys woke up. He stared at Omvendyn.

"Wakey wakey," Omvendyn said. "You going to do anything foolish? If not, I'll let you walk and ungag you, though I'll keep your hands tied."

Barakystys thought for a moment, then sagged and shook his head.

Omvendyn laughed. "You remember me, don't you?"

She pulled the gag off. Barakystys took a few deep breaths then said, "Yes, Priestess, I remember you. Are you punishing me and taking me to the Fish Chambers?"

"No. Somewhere much more interesting."

Barakystys listened to the small talk of the three women as they walked along Platan Street. Dawn broke, and the rain receded to seaborne drizzle. Luminous fungi in the Gardens to their left; empty houses with algae cushions bulging out of their front doors to the right. He still felt in shock.

"We're going into the Andromeda Quarter?" he asked Omvendyn.

She nodded. "On a mission."

"And you need… me?"

Omvendyn nodded again.

He said, "But I'm infertile."

Omvendyn frowned. "Think you're clever, do you? You know nothing, boy."

"But at the Spired Inn my partner Aqa –"

"You haven't got a partner any more," Omvendyn declared.

Barakystys shrugged. He remembered this woman well – hard as nails and single-minded. Among the Priestesses she had been notorious for ruthlessness. But if her plan involved penetrating the jungles of the Andromeda Quarter perhaps her ruthless streak had changed to madness. With Kray now collapsing, that was not unlikely.

He needed more information. He said, "I remember your sister Arvendyn too. She was linked to the cult of the Phallists, wasn't she? The rumour was, Taziqi the High Priestess sent her into the Andromeda –"

"Any more lip from you and the gag goes back on!"

Barakystys looked away. "Yes, Priestess."

They strode on. Crossing the River Kray by way of the Aum Bridge, they paused to survey what lay ahead. Though Jargonelle Street – cleared by red-garbed defenders, and free of lianas – lay before them, half-cleared Riverside to their right, they stood now at that liminal zone where Kray changed from urban decay to sprawling jungle. They had stepped upon Andromeda Quarter ground.

Barakystys listened. Like most Krayans, he had never been so close to this most enigmatic of the city's quarters. From twisted knolls arrayed with tropical trees he heard parrots screeching and the grunts of pandemic monkeys. The stacks and spires of millennia-old buildings reached for the heavens, some so tall their summits were invisible in rainclouds. Cobwebs lay like torn silver, mildew like black powder. Then came a thrum, a rumble, and a shiver through the ground.

"Local earth tremor," said Omvendyn. "Nothing to be concerned about."

"Which way?" Oqozara asked.

Omvendyn took a few deep breaths, then let out a sigh. "South down Riverside," she said. "The region between Jargonelle Street and the Galactic Port is just too tangled. Though there's more animals to the south, it should be an easier trek."

Oqozara and Meiryonyn led the way. Barakystys followed in silence, reflecting that at least his captor had done her homework – what little homework could be done about such a place. As the whoops of hunting spiders echoed down fern-choked alleys he cringed, recalling childhood tales written to scare. *Never* go down to the Andromeda Quarter…

At Peppermint Street they struck east, passing a number of defender groups hacking back the greenery. A few corpses lay half drenched, half eaten, all of them long since stripped of trinkets by the local revellers.

"What about cats?" Barakystys asked. "The Temple of Felis stands where eastern Andromeda meets Jessamine Street."

"I know where it is, thank you," Omvendyn grunted. "Oqozara, use a laser pistol if you see cats."

Oqozara grinned. "Quick and easy!" she said. "Don't

worry, no cat will scratch any of us."

Barakystys looked to his right. Far away he saw the Citadel tumulus, its illuminated pavements visible as a fog-shrouded glow above the warren of the Old Quarter. He glanced up through rents in the clouds to see the dark, brooding bulk of the Spaceflower.

He sighed. He was done for, surely. Too few emerged alive from treks into this part of the city.

"Where now?" he asked, as they stood aside to allow passing motorbikes access.

Omvendyn waited until the roar of the bike engines receded. She looked north, tapping fingers against her belt. "This zone seems a bit clearer," she murmured. "It says Bellicoze Street on that signpost." She examined a screen device, then added, "My map suggests the street leads towards the Ziggurat. I think we'll risk it. It's time to head inwards, off safe roads."

But as dusk fell and they approached the Ziggurat they faced an impassible barrier. From two great towers a glittering net of woven lianas blocked their path, like the jewelled web of some techno-spider.

"We've hacked our way far enough today," said Omvendyn. "We need to find a place to sleep."

Oqozara pointed at the remains of a house lying at the end of a short alley. "What about in there?"

"You two check it out."

Oqozara glanced at Meiryonyn, worry on her face.

"What did I hire you for, eh?" Omvendyn asked. "Get to work."

Barakystys watched as the pair entered the house. Light beams flashed as, with torches, they investigated. Then Oqozara emerged from the front doorway and waved them forward.

Indoors, all was dark and rotten. Fungi clothed the walls of most rooms, but a decaying conservatory at the rear seemed habitable. Yet what lay in the garden was too astonishing to ignore.

Barakystys studied it, his nose pressed to the algae-sheened glass. It appeared to be a vast flower petal, made from metal, untarnished yet clearly derelict. A number of animals had made nests, dens or other homes amongst its titanium folds.

"What in Kray's name is that?" said Meiryonyn.

Omvendyn glanced up at the sky. "Looks like a tiny Spaceflower petal."

"I was thinking the same thing," said Barakystys, turning around. "Perhaps it was a model that they used when building the Spaceflower."

"They, *they?*" Omvendyn replied. "What do you know about who built it?"

Barakystys shrugged. "Nothing much."

Omvendyn led them out into the garden. Barakystys noticed it was kempt, as if tended by autonomous machines. He began to feel anxious.

"This place is still inhabited," he said.

For once Omvendyn did not slap him down. She nodded, then tapped the great petal with a knife. The metal sang for ten seconds, like a cosmic bell.

At length Omvendyn said, "Our boy here could be correct. This reeks to me of the Phallists. I think they're nearby. I think we could have got lucky and this region is inhabited. Excellent. Exactly what I wished for."

"Who are you hoping to meet?" Barakystys asked. "Adherents of the Green Spermatozoon? Autonomous devices?"

Omvendyn laughed. "Perhaps you're a bit cleverer than I thought," she said. "Got a brain, have you? Good. We'll need it, maybe."

"You know the old tales, don't you?" Barakystys replied.

Omvendyn scowled, but then her expression softened. "Well… p'raps I'd like to hear what a *boy* knows of such tales."

"They say –"

"Who are these *they* you keep referring to?"

"Tale tellers, Priestess. Historians… Women."

Omvendyn grunted something, then turned her back. "Continue."

Barakystys said, "One day the Goddess was strolling across the firmament, just out for a walk, and she happened to notice a fungus spore shooting away from her towards her sister Seylene. The spore came from her omphalos. The Goddess tried to stop this spore from flying away – with her hand – but she couldn't, and it hit her sister. Then the spore began to grow, and nothing could stop it eating away at her sister… a kind of silicon leprosy. In due course Seylene was completely transformed into a flower – the Spaceflower. That's the origin of the Spaceflower, they… I mean, women say."

Omvendyn nodded. "Seylene is the ancient moon of this planet, the planet our Goddess personifies. Seylene used to be spherical. Some historians at my temple say the spore was the Silver Seed, that redemptive device flung from Kray in aeons past." She sighed. "We'll never know."

Barakystys, sensing her mood, decided it was time to take a risk. He said, "Arvendyn wanted to find the Silver Seed, didn't she? And you do too."

"What?"

"The Phallists are the last remaining link to the ancient religion of the Green Spermatozoon, who I heard were the people who made the Spaceflower."

Omvendyn grimaced. "Shut up with your guesswork."

Barakystys nodded. He knew now why Omvendyn needed a man in her group.

Omvendyn pondered all she had learned during the

exploration of the ruined house. It had once belonged to Phallists, judging by the murals they had uncovered behind fungal mats – masked and wearing breathing gear, Oqozara had cleared an entire room so that the theory could be confirmed. Omvendyn felt she was one step nearer an exit from Kray.

She looked up into the sky. Though she had not guessed the connection between this quarter and the Spaceflower, ancient tales known to priestesses of the Goddess had hinted as much. She smiled. Her guesses had been supported. In this quarter lay escape from Kray, via space. Off-planet was the only way out.

But in the morning, when she opened the front door, she saw a deputation awaiting her. At once she called for assistance.

A woman approached her; tall, tattooed and bald, and smelling of antiseptics. An artificial phallus and scrotum lay at her waist, decorated with amethyst shards and hung from a leather cord. Like her kin, she wore only green clothes, which confirmed her identity.

Oqozara ran to her side. "Priestess?"

Omvendyn gestured at the approaching woman. "Phallists," she said.

Hearing this, the tall woman frowned. "You know my kind?" she asked.

"I am none other than Omvendyn of the Temple of the Goddess. I know your kind indeed. But I seek knowledge. You possess that knowledge."

"This is our place," came the reply.

"And mine," Omvendyn replied. "For nearby lies the first temple of the Goddess. We are akin therefore. What is your name?"

The woman considered this question, then relaxed and replied, "Coryundror. Are you the sister of Arvendyn?"

"The same. Tell me, Coryundror… I saw a fragment of the Spaceflower in the garden behind this house. What is it?"

"Follow me to learn more."

Omvendyn hesitated. This was forward of the cultist. To Oqozara she whispered, "Guard me. Say nothing of the other two. The boy must remain an ace up my sleeve."

Oqozara nodded.

Coryundror led the way east, hacking a path through dense undergrowth. From the windows of ruined houses great white flowers emerged, dripping unguents to the ground, while high up on smashed roofs miniature hyenas prowled. The ground in places became hot, as mysterious underground processes divested themselves of surplus energy. Once, a strong tremor caused them to halt until, with a groan, the quake subsided. Chimneys toppled from distant roofs. They awaited calm, then continued.

In a bower guarded by steel palms Omvendyn found her knowledge. Astonished, she looked up at an enormous artefact preserved by the Phallists. It was in form an airborne ovoid, made of green metal, with a long tail, also green. But it was vast – clearly a vehicle. It looked in excellent condition. Upon studying the thing, Omvendyn thought she could divine its purpose.

But she realised she must not say too much too soon. She needed to feign ignorance. "This is a mighty machine," she said, "but surely it is inutile?"

"Oh no," Coryundror replied. "It will ascend."

"Then it epitomises a transformative technology?"

"We worship that aspect."

Omvendyn heard words passing into her mind's ear: *she happened to notice a fungus spore shooting away from her towards her sister Seylene. The spore came from her omphalos… it hit her sister… the spore began to grow, and nothing could stop it eating away at her sister… a kind of silicon leprosy. In due course Seylene was completely transformed into… the Spaceflower.*

Omvendyn nodded. "This is sacred ground indeed." She knelt, then bowed her head once at Coryundror and once at the great vehicle. "Oh vast and wondrous Goddess, bring truth to me via your strayed children, who wear their symbols at their waists. For this is a seminal moment. Praise be to you!"

Coryundror smiled, then also knelt, nodding once in the direction of the vehicle, then at Omvendyn. "You and I are akin," she said. "Then, only you two made it through the jungle?"

"How many of you are there?"

"Seven."

Omvendyn stood up. Four might overcome seven, she thought.

Barakystys sat down before Omvendyn. It perturbed him that there was no sign of the other two. "Don't you need guarding any more?" he asked. "Staying in this house is risky."

"Enough of your questions," Omvendyn replied. "There is something I need you to do. That you *will* do."

Hearing this, Barakystys realised he must not show one hint of rebellion. "Of course, Priestess," he said. "I'm yours to command."

"Good. There is just a chance that you may fall into a life of luxury, that no Krayan – least of all a man – could ever hope existed. There is just a chance…"

"Of escape?"

Omvendyn nodded. "You've guessed the score, then, for all your artlessness. We all wish to leave Kray this year. But some of us don't trust our so-called leaders."

"I trust you," Barakystys said.

Omvendyn gestured over her shoulder. "Back there, seven Phallists hold an extraordinary treasure. That old folk tale you told me was more than half true. A transformative technology as old as the roots of this city lives on, a remnant of the old religion of the Green Spermatozoon. The Phallists care for it. They use scaffolding to approach it. But I think, with your help, we could pilot that vehicle out of this city."

"Pilot?"

Omvendyn smiled. "That will be your job. The Phallists don't know I've got you. A real male… infertile or not, it doesn't matter. My guess is the vehicle will recognise you, and accept you."

"And was this your hope all along?"

Omvendyn nodded. "Of course, I knew nothing of the vehicle, but rumours of the Phallists live on in much Krayan lore. Long I wondered if such rumours might represent escape off-planet. Naturally, you have to know how to interpret old stories."

"Then you hope to escape and start anew…" He glanced at the ceiling. "… up there?"

"Indeed I do."

"But if I'm infertile," said Barakystys, "there won't be any children."

"If my guess is correct, we'll be able to return to the surface, for instance to the Cowhorn Tower."

Now Barakystys saw all of her plan. No wonder she did not want her two guards to know it. "I understand! Then I would be your pilot, not your inseminator."

"Exactly. So you will do what I wish, and to the letter?"

"Of course. I also want to survive."

Omvendyn leaned close, so that Barakystys smelled her mint-tinged breath. "Coryundror, the big cock, she won't want her precious green vehicle tampered with, so we will have to take it by force. That means you'll have to fight at our side."

"I will."

"Loyalty, Barakystys. You *swear* so?"

"I swear by the Goddess, whom I hold dear."

Omvendyn smiled and stood up, but Barakystys felt sick.

He had no option but to make the oath – he was a man of the Goddess. He *would* have to fight, he *would* have to pilot, he *would* have to accede to Omvendyn's insane wishes. In nine easy words he had sealed his fate.

Omvendyn checked every weapon before they departed the house. They had six in total. Because Oqozara and Meiryonyn were martial experts, she gave Barakystys her needle gun. He stared at it, astonished. She wanted to make him swear again, but she thought better of it. She was anxious: he had shown himself to be pliable. Her plan would succeed, with him at her side.

Outside the bower she met two of the Phallists – guards, she thought, with Coryundror most likely inside. She hesitated. She would have to down these two first, then take on the other five. Not ideal. Noise would warn Coryundror of the attack. But there was no choice.

Without warning she raised her pistol and fired. The energy beam knocked down both women, rendering them unconscious. What mattered now was the other Phallists. She sprinted towards the bower, calling for the others to follow.

But inside, a surprise awaited. Coryundror stood behind a transparent shield, her kin in a line behind her. Omvendyn fired at the shield, but the beam bounced away: light off a mirror.

"Pull down the shield!" Omvendyn ordered her hirelings.

Oqozara and Meiryonyn stepped forward, but they appeared uncertain. Coryundror laughed, taking a rifle from the rack beside her. "Did you think we would risk our sacred space?" she asked.

Omvendyn said nothing.

"We knew a little about Arvendyn," Coryundror continued, "but nothing about you. Phallists take no risks. We've learned not to. Lower your weapons!"

Omvendyn glanced over her shoulder as the metal palms of

the bower turned and walked forward, their razor sharp leaves whirling as they approached.

"I ask that you capture them," Coryundror told the autonomous machines. "If they resist, slice them up. But not the man."

Barakystys sat at the side of the bower as twilight arrived. Despite Omvendyn's failure, the three women were alive, albeit in a cell; and he was free. Moreover, because he had not had a chance to use his weapon the Phallists had not seen it. But neither had they searched him. He smiled to himself. Men were not permitted to bear arms in Kray, so Coryundror had assumed he was defenceless.

Yet she and the other Phallists treated him with something approaching awe. He was a man, a manifestation of the abstract notion they worshipped. Could he use that fact to save himself and return to the Spired Inn?

As dusk fell and the yellow anjiqs of the bower flickered into life, Coryundror approached him, sitting at his side. She offered him a plate of stewed yams, but he turned it down. "I'm not hungry," he lied.

"They're not poisoned. Do you think they are?"

The aroma of the meal tempted him. "Perhaps."

"Why would we kill you now? You've been free to roam all day."

"I don't trust you. How could I? You told me not to leave the bower." He paused. "Anyway, what do you want me for?"

"It's been decades since we saw a live man in the Andromeda Quarter."

Barakystys shivered. He did not like the sound of that. "I don't know what you mean."

"Don't you?"

He looked away. "What happened to the last man here?"

"He had a good life."

"You're cultists," Barakystys said, "toying with me, like cats with mice."

"*Never* mention cats to us. Not here."

Barakystys nodded. The Temple of Felis was not so far away. "I apologise," he said. "I spoke without thinking."

Coryundror handed him the plate. Picking up the spoon, he tasted a mouthful.

"It's good," he said.

Coryundror stood up. "Finish it all. Then, when night arrives, I'll show you something."

Again Barakystys shuddered. Though her manner was neutral, there was venom in her words.

Who should he take his chances with? He could not escape the bower alone. If he stayed with the cultists, his fate would likely be grim. The religion of the Green Spermatozoon came from the time when chemicals in the environment feminised males, leading to a macabre imbalance between men and women. Most likely these Phallists would kill him with misplaced benevolence. That left Omvendyn and her insane plan.

Frogs and toads began their nocturnal songs as twilight became night. The interior of the bower was warm, fans at its circumference sending a pleasant breeze across the place. Barakystys watched two of the Phallists tending to their still half-conscious kin. Coryundror and the other pair sat nearby, playing cards.

He stood up and stretched, feigning relaxation. Coryundror glanced up, but seemed unconcerned. Barakystys felt the metal needle gun in his coat pocket. It was loaded with two dozen needles, Omvendyn had explained.

Too risky to trust these weird women. Their cult was twisted, though they held him in reverence. He had to keep to his oath.

He strolled to the rear of the bower, where lay the cell. As he passed it he saw that its door was closed with a metal latch. He saw no lock, no electronic security. Low tech. He walked on, as if bored.

The trio first, then.

A few yards away from them he took out the needle gun and sprayed a single round. Three needles hit. Coryundror, aghast, stood up and took a tube from her pocket, raising it as if to fire an energy beam, but already the chemical cocktail in the needles paralyzed her. She fell, as did the other two.

The remaining Phallists jumped to their feet and drew weapons. Barakystys dived behind a stack of pyuters, then crawled to the cell. With a bamboo cane he reached out to unlatch the door, which in response squeaked and opened a little.

But now the two active Phallists were prepared for a fight. Barakystys crawled on his stomach to the cell door and said, "Two still unaccounted for. I think they can see the cell, though. Crawl out before it's too late."

Moments later all four of them lay behind the pyuter stack.

"What now?" Barakystys asked Omvendyn. "The metal palms are quiet. They must be voice sensitive. Lucky I downed Coryundror…"

The Priestess turned to Oqozara. "What do you think? Though we outnumber them, they have energy weapons."

"Leave it to us," Oqozara replied.

Barakystys knew the pair were unarmed. He handed over his needle gun, which Oqozara took. "A dozen needles left," he told her.

Oqozara nodded, then whispered to Meiryonyn. The pair crawled to the far side of the pyuter stack, where Oqozara pointed to the transparent shield, which remained standing – and not too distant. Barakystys thought he could see what they were planning.

Meiryonyn made a run for the shield, ducking and diving in

an attempt to avoid being hit. The two Phallists fired, but both missed, bamboozled by the jerky motion of their opponent. Moments later Meiryonyn stood behind the screen: safe. She grabbed a rifle from the rack and armed it. At once the Phallists crouched down, but too late. Oqozara stood up and fired a second spray of needles – an all-or-nothing shot. Yet luck was on her side. Two needles hit. Moments later the Phallists collapsed.

Omvendyn sprinted forward, and with her hirelings disarmed the Phallists. Minutes later all seven lay inside the cell.

Omvendyn turned to Barakystys. "Well done," she said. "You will be rewarded for your faithfulness."

Omvendyn stood alongside Barakystys outside the bower. Something about the night seemed wrong to her.

"What is different?" she asked.

"I don't know," he replied. "But the light has changed."

Oqozara and Meiryonyn approached. Oqozara said, "What's that in the sky?"

Omvendyn gazed up at the heavens. Drizzle fell, but it was more like mist from receding clouds. Through ragged wisps she saw an illuminated object hanging over the city.

"It is the Spaceflower!" she said.

They stared at it in silence. For uncounted millennia the Spaceflower had hung dark above Kray, enigmatic, wreathed in Goddess lore, a creation, it seemed, of ancient transformative technology out of control. Yet now the fine black lines that everyone had thought to be shadows, or some kind of folding in the vast structure, were illuminated, shining with blues, indigo and purples, here and there pulsing with white and gold. It was as if the Spaceflower had come alive.

"The Citadel is dark," Barakystys said.

From the bower they could see the top of the tumulus. In

normal circumstances it was bright, its many plastic streets illuminated by electronic activity within. Now all that activity appeared to have transferred to the Spaceflower.

And she heard constant gunfire.

"Something dreadful has happened," she said, "some devious plan of the Portreeve I expect. It sounds like gun battles all over the Citadel Quarter. Anarchy must reign there. But how can the Citadel be dark? Has the Portreeve abrogated her agreement with the city?"

"What agreement?" asked Barakystys.

"To save us!"

"She lied," said Oqozara. "They all did. She and the Red Brigade have saved themselves."

Omvendyn cursed. She felt desperate now. "Then we will do at once what I said we would do," she declared. "Damn all leaders! We four shall fly that green vehicle to the Spaceflower and demand to be let in."

"Now?" asked Barakystys.

"You swore to!" Omvendyn replied, turning to face him.

He hesitated. "And I will, Priestess. Well... let us see what doors the vehicle has."

They ran back into the bower and headed for the vehicle. "There is a portable tower at the rear of the bower," Omvendyn said, pointing to a rickety pile of scaffolding. "They must have used that to clean and care for the vehicle. Its green metal is shiny, as if new. This is the aspect they worshipped – the transformative part. That vehicle will fly into orbit, I know it. You two! Pull the scaffolding to the thing so that Barakystys can ascend and locate the way in."

The two women did as they were told, then Barakystys began to ascend. But although he hesitated Omvendyn felt no doubt that the man would follow his oath. He would pilot this thing.

Through a monocular she watched his progress. For a few

moments he adjusted his trousers, and she was surprised to see him glance down at her, red-faced, then manoeuvre himself as though trying to conceal an erection.

"Get on with it!" she shouted. "Is there a door?"

"It's playing with my mind," he called back. "I can't go on."

"Find me a door!" she yelled. "And *quickly*."

He turned away, so that all she could see was his back. But because of his embarrassment and his words she knew she was on the right path. Excitement rose within her. She *did* need a man to pilot this vehicle. Therefore it contained a mind of sorts, artificial and nonsentient like those ridiculous entities worshipped at the Temple of the Dead Spirits, but a mind nonetheless – one attuned to the Goddess and her green planet, in fact. Through pheromone activity or some other bio-trick it was now investigating the male newcomer. Good! Her plan was going to work.

Soon she saw a black rectangle appear in the green metal.

"A way in!" Barakystys shouted.

Omvendyn gestured at her hirelings. "Follow me!" she cried.

They clambered up the scaffolding then followed Barakystys into the vehicle. At once Omvendyn heard groaning and noise as of metal grating against metal, so she peered out, to see the top of the bower parting, its segmented sections pulling back like lotus flower petals opening at dawn.

"The bower is part of the whole," she said. "My guess is that it has opened to allow the vehicle to ascend. Stay inside, all of you. Remain calm."

Before her lay a circular chamber set with couches. Control panels floated on whisker-thin perspex rods. The place smelled of musk.

Barakystys looked confused. "But how can I fly this?" he asked. He pointed to the control panels, adding, "I don't know any of this."

"We'll work it out together," she replied.

She forced him down onto one of the couches, then sat next to him. On springy rods a control panel leaned forward, as if aware of their presence.

"See?" she said. "The vehicle *knows* we're here. This whole place does. Because of your presence, we're welcome. So we'll be able to set a course for the Spaceflower and fly there." She laughed. "We're going to *do* it! We really are. Escape the city…"

The control panels were diagramatic, arranged in sections: ground, vehicle, propulsion, destination. By touching various virtual buttons she was able to work out the control patterns used. Red colour indicated off or not set, with green to indicate on and active. Each virtual section represented real technology.

"You have to sense the metaphor," she told Barakystys. "This is a sacred vehicle, so it utilises the iconography of the original religion. As a Priestess of the Goddess, I recognise a lot of that iconography." She chuckled. "Could hardly be easier."

"Will we go now?" he asked.

With a forefinger she linked the propulsion system to the vehicle itself, visible on the control panel as a sperm-shaped icon.

She activated the entire virtual array, tapping once: red to green.

"Yes," she replied.

As he lay back on the couch, Barakystys felt events rushing by, out of control, bizarre, impossible to understand. He grasped the metaphor of the vehicle and he saw exultation in Omvendyn's eyes, but he did not think he was going to be saved. This was Kray's final year, and everybody would die.

Humanity had created the conditions for its own demise –

that fact was well known.

Gravity changed, pushing him into the soft couch. Yet it was no push of force; it was light, variable, carefree, as though the vehicle, via incomprehensible technology, was doing its best to care for them. He pondered what he had heard of ancient tales: the great achievements of civilisation, the great machines, the great minds inside those machines… all for nothing. All in the past, all ancient… and if machines lingered in the city, they were too difficult to use, or too dangerous. This vehicle would surely crash.

Though he lay inside the ancient space vehicle he felt neither fear nor awe. His was a body controlled by another. He was flotsam in time. Irrelevant.

A voice brought him back to reality.

"We're slowing down."

He felt light as a feather.

Omvendyn leaned over him, slapping his cheek once. "Wake up! Zero gravity. We'll remain belted into these couches for safety."

"Will the vehicle be our envoy?"

"No," she replied. "I'll speak for us. I know what to say."

"To the Portreeve?"

"Yes, to that red bitch. She won't dare ignore me."

Barakystys glanced around. The other two women lay half-conscious in their couches. Omvendyn's face looked determined – angry, even. The chamber lay bright green and twinkling around them. He turned to see a door at the rear, which he supposed led to the tail systems. A sigil above the door showed a cylinder with a window in it. For a few moments he pondered what that might signify, before Omvendyn's voice broke into his thoughts.

"Look! On the main screen. A *face*."

Barakystys' vision swam as the strange conditions affected his body. He felt nauseous. "Is it the Portreeve?" he asked.

"No, it's something weird. A tall woman with a horse's head… and a mane, and hooves. That's some nice silk finery though, and even a ruff. Enamelled belt, a string of pearls…"

"You could try to find a voice channel. Ask her who she is. She must be inside the Spaceflower, perhaps she's the door warden."

For a few moments Omvendyn pressed virtual buttons, until a click sounded.

"Can you hear me?" she asked.

The woman on the screen replied, "My, but who are you?"

"Omvendyn of the Goddess. These are my hirelings. And you are?"

"I am Laspetosyne. Why have you ascended?"

"To join you. You do work for the Portreeve?"

Laspetosyne laughed. "Girl, of course not."

Barakystys saw the colour drain from Omvendyn's face. "Then," Omvendyn said, "the Portreeve and the Red Brigade aren't in there with you?"

"The Portreeve is an organic creature," came the reply, "like all others of your species. We are electronic."

"We?"

"Me and my noophyte kin. This is our way station. You are not welcome. There is no environment for you here, because you have bodies. I will send your craft away now so that it burns up in the atmosphere. Your deaths will be swift."

"No!" Omvendyn cried. "We came here to join you!"

"As I explained – we exist in virtual environments. You do not. Your planet is your home."

"But Kray is about to *die*. There is no other haven left. All is green poison and choking mire, from north pole to south."

"Then in earlier aeons you should have lived your lives with more care and understanding. Goodbye."

The connection faded. The screen died.

At once Barakystys felt gravity changing, his body moving

as if propelled by an invisible hand. Oqozara began to wail. Meiryonyn prayed.

But Barakystys could think of one thing only: he lay inside a vehicle of the Green Spermatozoon. If the Phallists' metaphor was true to biology…

As Omvendyn lay motionless beside him he wrestled with his belt buckle, then tumbled out of the couch.

"It's no use," Omvendyn murmured. "This is the end. Strange creatures have bested us from our own destiny. Humanity is doomed."

"Not me," Barakystys muttered to himself.

Already the chamber felt warmer: heat from friction as at speed the vehicle sank into the atmosphere. At the rear of the chamber he hammered on the door.

It opened. Before him lay a twisting chamber, far too long to see in its entirety and filled with glowing devices. Yet this was the tail of the sperm. It should fall off. It should fall away from the vehicle…

A single nook in the outer wall awaited him, soft inside – lined with ermine – and labelled with the cylinder/window sigil. This therefore was an auxiliary pod. He struggled into it as, burning up, the main vehicle bucked and shook.

Then a sudden, sickening crash: a clunk, a jolt: then calm. Separation?

He prayed to the Goddess.

Time passed.

After a while gravity threw him this way and that, but the tail section did not heat up. Calm returned.

Then another jolt, a bang… silence.

Had he landed?

He did not know.

The tail section lay quiescent around him, its devices now dark. He crawled out of the nook and kicked the door open.

Dim light, the stink of methane and sewage… and the

unmistakable colour of copper. He struggled out then looked over his shoulder. Like a green python the vehicle's tail section had wrapped itself around the lower column of the Cowhorn Tower.

But of course, he thought. Where else?

He examined the tower's pleasure garden, but saw no immediate danger. All lay at peace. Dawn was close: a new day. And he must not waste a single day of his life now.

He hurried along the path leading out of the garden until he found himself on Sphagnum Street, from where a damp journey north began. But half an hour later he found himself on Morte Street, hale, unmolested, with the aquamarine lamps of the Spired Inn nearby.

He opened the inn's front door, cleaned himself up in the green zone, then entered the common room.

Standing behind the bar, Dhow-lin stared at him. "Where the hell have you been?"

He replied, "Is Aqa here? Is she safe?"

"Yes. What's going on?"

He sighed. He relaxed. He sat down on a chair. "My tale," he said, "is lengthy and surprising…"

Memory Seed

Green city.

To the north, nothing remained except piles of rubble indistinguishable from natural outcrops of rock, covered with moss and grass, hidden by bush and tree, dark green, emerald, olive, occasionally yellow or white in the summer rain. Northern plains were criss-crossed with animal tracks. Through these uplands a river passed, flowing towards cliffs, becoming a waterfall, then flowing on until it met the glowing sea.

Further south, ruins stood like teeth in a skeleton, green with algae and red with rust. West of the river, a verdigris-covered tower stood unchanged by the plants. East of the river stood a slimmer tower. In the far south there rose a single tongue of black plastic, dotted here and there with birds' nests. In these flowered, colourful places butterflies fluttered, great quantities of them produced by the heat and the profusion of nectar. There were tiny meadows filled to bursting with cowslips, ferns, hogweed, and also with nettles and docks boasting leaves as large as a water lily's.

Southern parts remained flooded, slime and algae slapped across brick and stone, covering floods with scum. Here and there tiny leaves showed where other plants had found a roothold. Insects swarmed across these turbid pools and lakes, mosquitoes and daddy-longlegs, flies and boaters. Beetles swam. Larvae choked the multitude of growing spaces. In Eastcity there was a plague of fleas. Food was plentiful.

Eventually, when the meat provided by the year's glut of corpses became too bad to eat, the hawks and vultures departed for further fields. Time passed by. Leaves took on bright colours, red and yellow, orange and brown, while animal life, particularly in the south, burst into new living spaces, caves once houses, vaults once cellars, eyries and ledges.

Gases bubbled from fermenting vegetation while from rotting things anaerobic bacteria produced more.

A great yield of seeds ensued. From all types of plant seeds of every description grew; hard brown cases on some, the size of rats, small black motes on others. Whole pastures were transformed into white down, rising like smoke at the touch of a breeze. These pastures were undisturbed by human footsteps. In other places, especially near the Gardens, some plants produced purple fans, small glittering daggers, arrays of blunt pins.

As the year progressed, the fruit dropped or rotted or was eaten and burrowed into by insects; great green wasps with lethal stings, also spiders and the occasional bee. Squirrels harvested, and, on the ground, deer and rabbits, dogs and foxes enjoyed the spree.

To the south, water-plants produced their fruits, to be consumed by fish and insects, voles and weasels. The stinking pools merged into stinking lakes, so thick in places that even a wind could not disturb their glutinous surfaces. In other areas these pools were alive with insects and grubs.

The temperature began to fall. Rain abated into showers. Floods settled and the remains of buildings began to show through, already eroded by weather.

Soon green was muted, especially in the south. In the north, grass plains and bogs expanded, the bushes and trees growing among them bare and brown and whipped by the wind. Hibernating animals began preparing their hides. Birds flocked in high places, many using the extended horns of the green-stained tower, others clustering around fallen pylons and the mounts of solar mirrors now crumbling into rust. In dense flocks they waited, until internal calls sent them flying across the ocean.

Snow fell. Frosts froze over the floods, encasing dead leaves and living tendrils in ice. Cracks and snaps from rock and brick resounded through the city, and buildings were flattened. Snow settled on the ruins and cracked branches.

In the north, deer foraged; also rabbits and badgers, and even an occasional bear. Birds of prey wheeled overhead, many with new white plumage.

Southward there was little movement. The ice ponds and lakes were quiet. Elsewhere, robins and sparrows fluttered, and there were rustlings under the snow and debris from scavenging voles and hares, stoats and mink. To the east cat families foraged far and wide, hunting with their envenomed claws, scrabbling through the snow, and padding, backs arched, along the remains of sandstone walls and across precarious roofs.

More snow fell. Ice stalactites clothed the city, often encasing within their lengths rotten plant material. Huge drifts built up in those few alleys and streets left as such. More buildings collapsed as more snow flurries danced through the air.

And then, as spring approached, there were hints of new life.

The Green Realm Below

Through the rain, Kytanquil could see the aquamarine lamps of the Spired Inn like corpse lights floating around a mausoleum. The inn was a tall, domed structure with a single door, to which she ran as the wind blew drizzle into her face. It was the last centre of culture in this northerly district of the dying city of Kray.

And it was her home, for Kytanquil was the daughter of Oq-Ziq, notorious thief and local ambassador for the jannitta culture, and Balgydyal, notorious lech and ambassador for nothing.

Inside the hall she stuffed her boots into an antiseptic bin, pulled off her film protectives and dressed in a white shift and slippers that she withdrew from her kit, belting the shift with string and inflating the slippers with a minipump. She opened the door to the common room and strolled in. Dark alcoves of oak surrounded her, their carven sides flickering as a multitude of giant candles sputtered and hissed. A few locals drank dooch from tankards. At the bar she saw the innkeeper, Dhow-lin, a crusty old woman dressed in the traditional smock of her aamlon culture.

This was through force of circumstance a cosmopolitan inn, where melancholy Krayans mingled with exotic jannitta, who were in turn mellowed by the intense, almost elegiac musicality of the aamlon. Kytanquil, never quite at home with any of these cultures, nevertheless found the mixture a comfort, for her personality was not sober, not passionate, nor yet profound. She was a drifter. Not a loner, but a misfit.

Her appearance caused a trio of priestesses from the Goddess Temple to stare at her. She was unusually tall, her short bleached hair slicked back with antiseptic gel, her sad dark eyes – identical to her mother's – like anti-lamps in a bright face. She ignored the priestesses, and they returned to their whispered conversation.

Dhow-lin greeted her. "Come along. Drink?"

Kytanquil approached the bar and said, "Is she in?"

"No. Out raiding some unsafe homes wired off by defenders this morning. Four or five families forced south to the refugee streets."

"Hmmm." Kytanquil nodded to the bottles of mootsflosser. She enjoyed a special relationship with Dhow-lin on account of her mother, which allowed her such luxuries as credit and free board. "Make it a big glass."

Swilling the creamy liqueur around her goblet, she surveyed the clientele. Apart from the priestesses, all were locals. She turned back to the bar, only to see Dhow-lin's hand waving a slip of plastic at her. "I forgot, this message came for you."

Only one symbol had been printed on the fragment, a red splotch looking like a leaf. She did not recognise it. But her bracelet did.

The bracelet had been a present from a mysterious relative, an object she had owned since her rite of puberty, a wide bracelet of gold, copper and silicon with an object embedded in it resembling a soft emerald. Now that dark jewel glowed, and as she waved the slip at it bright green beams burst out. One of the decorative frills beside the jewel moved to become a slit, and before she knew it the slip was being ingested by the bracelet, until all that was left was the smell of lavender incense. The whole incident lasted just seconds.

"What did it do?" Dhow-lin asked.

"I don't know," Kytanquil replied, "I had no idea it was active."

Dhow-lin looked unimpressed. "It's trouble, that's certain. Throw it. It's useless for bartering and it ain't a weapon."

"It is an heirloom," Kytanquil pointed out.

"An heirloom that even Kray's greatest cat-burglar can't identify," Dhow-lin scoffed, adding in a sing-song voice, "That's dangerous."

"My mother doesn't know everything."

Dhow-lin's response was cut short when another slit opened up and a translucent orange wafer slid out. It fell to the bar with a metallic plink.

Dhow-lin gasped. "A Garden fret!"

Kytanquil did not recognise the phrase, but she understood the shock in Dhow-lin's voice. "A what?" she asked.

After a pause, Dhow-lin said, "A call from the secret inhabitants of the Garden. They want to meet you."

"Why?"

"Nobody but them can know, can they? They're the ultimate secret society, older by far than the Phallists, more skilled than the Club of Shadowy Thieves. You better go."

"But where exactly?" Kytanquil asked.

"Go to the Greenhouses, that's my advice. But don't tell nobody I said so."

And so Kytanquil found herself outside the Spired Inn, looking south, wondering what to do.

Only one thing to do. Prepare weapons and locate the Greenhouses.

The Garden was shunned by all in Kray; too dangerous to cross, with its sucking marshes, carnivorous plants and razor flowers that leaped from the ground to cut out the eyes of the unwary. So Kytanquil followed its southern wall, until she saw the single safe area, a zone of grass by a gate, at its far end the twinkling panes of the Greenhouses. She called out her name and purpose, but nobody answered. Slowly, she walked up to the nearest Greenhouse, and entered.

A man stood up from behind a wooden box. Kytanquil jumped, one hand at the dagger on her belt. He was dressed in a leather apron and boots, under these muddy protectives rough garments of denim. She could not see his eyes, for they were hidden behind wraparound sunglasses so polished they reflected every gleam of candle and lamp. When he smiled, she saw teeth filed to points.

"Hello," he said in a deep voice. "Who are you?"

In silence Kytanquil held up the orange wafer.

"Ah," he said. "Then welcome to our realm! I am Awanshyva."

"Who are you?"

"The Advocate of the Plants."

Kytanquil looked at him, dread making her skin crawl. Bloodstains marked his clothes, and his teeth were decayed to the colour orange. "Why did you call for me?" she asked.

He seemed not to have heard her. "I am ashamed to admit that in my youth I did eat plants. But now I am wholly carnivorous. The destruction of Kray, which is the final city of humankind, is an end I pray for every night. Ah, yes."

Kytanquil cringed and took a step back. Time to depart.

"But there is need of you," Awanshyva said, his voice suddenly loud, "for you wear the bracelet of –"

"This bracelet?" Kytanquil interrupted, raising her arm. "You know what it is?"

"Not yet. Now is the time to find out. Follow me."

He turned, and like a zombie began to trudge deeper into the greenhouse. Kytanquil hesitated, then gripped tight the handle of her dagger and followed, thinking that they would go deeper into the Garden. So she was surprised when he stooped to pull up a metal cover in the earth, then dropped into the chamber below. She was left peering down into the pale green gloom, in which Awanshyva stood like a troglodyte, his wraparound shades reflecting the peppermint light provided by countless tiny fungi.

"Come," he said.

Kytanquil felt torn. Afraid of the man, yet impelled by the curiosity in her drifting spirit, she hesitated on the brink of the hole, before gripping her dagger still tighter and jumping down. "Don't even think of touching me," she warned. "I was trained in steel combat by Oq-Ziq, my mother."

"That is a lie," Awanshyva countered.

Shocked by his certainty, Kytanquil found no reply.

"Dead, you are useless," Awanshyva remarked. "Now follow me, and please do not fear."

So Kytanquil followed. At the end of the chamber stood the remains of a door, which Awanshyva smashed aside with his fists. He led the way into a tunnel that after a hundred yards opened out into a chamber filled with rotten wood. Luminous orange and green fungi lit the place. At the further end lay another manhole cover, which Awanshyva prised open. A ladder of rusting iron led down into blackness. Kytanquil took a flashlight from her kit and peered into the depths, but it was too deep for her weak beam to penetrate. A claustrophobia born in the bottomless pit enveloped her.

Without a word, Awanshyva began to clamber down the ladder, leaving Kytanquil no option but to follow. She descended miner style: one hand behind, one hand in front of the ladder. Occasionally she would stop to close her eyes and draw a few deep breaths. The cold was intense.

After some time she heard boots striking a wet floor. She pointed the flashlight down to see a wide ledge damp with slime. Stepping off the ladder she kept hold of one rung, for the lip of the ledge was a sheer drop into blackness that even Awanshyva avoided.

"Are we here?"

Her voice reverberated in discrete echoes.

"No."

Slowly Awanshyva walked along the ledge. Rusting shards of metal stuck out from the wall, here and there plastered with red algae and the pale eggs of some subterranean crustacean. Slime dripped upon them from stalactites that twisted like questing tentacles. Kytanquil shivered, her reserve of bravery reaching its end.

Awanshyva led the way into another series of rooms, these carved from the rock with chisels, or so it seemed from the deeply gouged surfaces. Puddles of stinking water reflected the flashlight beam. Occasionally small green creatures would leap from these puddles and scuttle away, screeching with rage. In the last room Awanshyva pulled up another cover, then let himself into the hole. Kytanquil dropped down after him, to find another room, and another manhole.

They dropped into a room lit by blue fungi, glued to the walls in stripes as if they had dripped from the coving over the centuries. A smell of dead meat made Kytanquil retch. They hurried on into another tunnel, leading down, the slime on the floor making them slip and slide.

In desperation Kytanquil whispered, "How much further?"

"We are almost there."

At the end of the tunnel lay a cavern, its roof a single dome of blue fungi, so that for a few seconds Kytanquil had to squint, until her eyes became used to the illumination. A single column lay central, surrounded by items of junk, litter, fungi, and pale creatures like rats, with whiskers longer than their own bodies.

Kytanquil jumped. Three people walked from behind the column.

They were naked, their skin deep green, their black eyes defocused, with matted hair and black lips. Awanshyva turned to her and said, "These are three of the Slow People."

Kytanquil took a step back, so that he stood between her

and the creatures. "Ugh, what are they?"

"In the Green Quarter, deep now under cushions of fungi and twisted vines, lies the Venus Heart, an ancient plant that thinks. But it lives on a different time scale. A minute of its time is a year of ours. Its winter is our ice age. Certain personages need to communicate with the Venus Heart –"

"Wait, wait," Kytanquil interrupted, "I didn't come to this Goddess-forsaken pit to hear a lecture. What's this to do with me?"

"Those of the secret societies –"

"But *you're* one of them."

"I am the Advocate of the Plants, the seed of communication used by the societies when they wish to interact with the outside world. This is why they sent you the Garden fret. You are the one who will communicate with the Slow People, who will in turn communicate with the Venus Heart, who –"

"I doubt it very much," Kytanquil retorted.

After a pause Awanshyva observed, "It is true you cannot be forced." There was no menace in his voice.

"That's right. I won't be told to do anything."

"Do you wish to escape Kray?" Awanshyva asked.

"Yes! But I'm verging on reveller. What's the point in looking? It's the final year."

Awanshyva considered this, then said, "A year on your time scale maybe. But suppose you were offered the chance of life on another scale?"

"How? And who by, the secret societies of the Garden?"

"Perhaps."

"They're only people, probably religious zealots who think they've found the answer, just like those of the Temple of Dead Spirits, or of the Goddess for that matter."

Awanshyva nodded, and a cruel smile came to his lips. "I do not recall describing those of the secret societies as human."

Kytanquil said nothing. She had not considered the possibility of pyutons inhabiting the depths of the Garden, but now it seemed obvious, since the entire rotting green heart of Kray was inimical to human life. And this might also explain the references to longevity.

She replied, "I don't think I want anything to do with this. Take me back to the surface."

"Are you certain that is what you want?"

"Yes."

Awanshyva considered for a moment, then said, "Ah, so you wish to die along with the city."

Kytanquil sighed. She wanted to live. She wanted to survive. The dilemma that faced her was one of life and death. She wished she was somewhere else, in a quiet, warm inn, with people she knew and a glass of baqa in her hand.

"I'm not prepared to do dangerous things," she said. "These Slow People might kill me. How can I live on a different time scale to the one biologically programmed in me?"

"I see that I must show you more," Awanshyva remarked.

"More?"

"It was hoped that experience of the Slow People would be enough to convince you of the importance of your task."

"And?"

"We must return to the Garden."

Kytanquil did not like the sound of this. "And then?"

"Another meeting. And then your decision."

They departed.

Back in Awanshyva's greenhouse Kytanquil asked what would happen next. He replied, "You have two choices. Either you journey into the heart of the Garden and meet the secret society who charged me with bringing you here, or one of them comes to meet you. The former option would be the best for us all."

"I'll take the latter."

Without a word, Awanshyva turned to a panel of controls on one of the planting benches. It glowed yellow under the warmth of his hands, causing his wraparound shades to glitter with reflections like motes of sunlight. She thought she heard him muttering under his breath, as if speaking to it, but the patter of rain upon the panes above her head drowned out the sound. Then he jerked his head up, as if he had heard a noise.

"One comes," he said.

Unnerved, Kytanquil said, "What, already?"

"It will be here soon."

Kytanquil did not like the sound of that.

So they waited. After half an hour red and green lights outside the greenhouse indicated the arrival of guests. The rear door of the greenhouse opened and Kytanquil was confronted by something she had never seen before, not even in her worst nightmare.

In fact it was two beings. Standing beside an irregular lump of machinery blackened as if by fire, yet twinkling with red indicator lamps, was a grey-skinned human, eyes half closed, lips black, wearing a filthy robe and ripped boots. She – or he – was bald, with a limp body and none of the vitality Kytanquil associated with normal folk. But it was the grey skin that made her feel sick, marked as it was with livid bruises and scars as if from many operations. This person grasped two handles at the back of the machine and wheeled it forwards; and the castors squeaked like tortured rodents.

The pair stood before Kytanquil. Nervously, she addressed the grey person. "I gather you wanted to speak with me."

Awanshyva cleared his throat, leaned towards her, and whispered, "It would be better if you addressed your remarks to the pyuton, not the pyuton's chauffeur."

Kytanquil stared at the lump of metal. Now it was closer she could see the lenses and grilles of its sense organs, and the twisted loudspeaker that served to project its voice. Appalled, she shivered, finding herself unable to speak.

In a buzzing voice the pyuton said, "We meet at last, Kytanquil. I have looked forward to this meeting for some decades."

"You have?"

"Oh, yes. Your family is known to us."

Again Kytanquil shivered. "Why?"

"You are the daughter of Oq-Ziq, who was the daughter of Jizharaq and Nijdeere-lin. The traits of your family intrigue us, as do the tales of courage, intellect, wisdom and gall."

Kytanquil did not know what to make of this. Pyutons of course could live for centuries. Had her family been watched for so long? "What exactly do you want of me?"

The pyuton replied, "It was I who ensured that a certain bracelet was given to you at your rite of puberty. It was I who asked Awanshyva to bring you into the Garden. You see, Kytanquil, I am one of the six members of the Association for the Promotion of the Chlorophyll Age. We wish to speak with the Venus Heart, that ancient entity, half plant, half machine – so it is said – extant in the Green Quarter. To do this we need to converse with the Slow People. To do that, we need one brave volunteer. You, in fact."

"And if I refuse?"

"The time for refusal is now past."

Kytanquil retorted, "No it is not," and took a step back.

"Tell her, Awanshyva," said the pyuton.

Awanshyva said, "Now you have seen one of members of the Garden's secret societies, you are bound by their rules. To refuse is to die."

"But you gave me no choice!"

"Death offers you no choice. That was why it was not

necessary for me to tell you what would happen if you refused."

Kytanquil felt she had been trapped by powers wholly out of her control. She blustered, "You can't force me to do anything."

"But we can," said the pyuton. "However there will be no need for anything as vulgar as physical force. Our reward will be more than sufficient."

"Oh, yes?"

"Like all Krayans, you wish to survive the demise of this last human city. There are two options. One is to escape Kray. Such a feat is impossible, as far as we know. The other is to escape death."

Kytanquil did not believe this. "Immortality?"

"You might call it that. One species of immortality can be obtained from the Venus Heart. Our offer is this. If you become the actuator of our plan, we shall allow you to share the immortality of the Venus Heart."

"I don't understand," Kytanquil said. "Why don't you fetch this immortality yourself?"

"All pyuton expeditions have failed because the Venus Heart can detect the many varieties of sentient being in Kray. Only the Slow People have overcome its hostility. That is why a human being must go with the Slow People to converse with the Venus Heart. That human being, Kytanquil, is you."

"I'll be killed."

"No you won't. You will be a Slow Person."

"Never!"

Silence fell. Then Awanshyva said, "You are one already."

Kytanquil sat next to her mother in the Spired Inn and sobbed, "They told me I'm a Slow Person. What have they done to me?"

"You can't be one of them," Oq-Ziq said, "because you're

speaking to me now. The Slow People, so I've heard, can't talk or interact with us normal people because they're devoted to plants. That's why they're green. There are many folk tales about them from the north of the city, where they're occasionally seen." She paused to wipe the tears away from her daughter's eyes. "Don't worry. They were just trying to coerce you into something. The fact that they let you get away after all those threats means they aren't serious. You stay here for a while. I'll look after you."

Kytanquil departed for her room, a small attic at the top of the inn, where she lit a fire, grabbed a bottle of red brandy and a glass, and lay back on her bed. After a while she pulled the sheets over her body and fell asleep.

Over the next few days all seemed well. Nobody came to the Spired Inn to disturb her, there were no messages, nor any visitors.

Then one morning she noticed something different about her body. Everyone suffered from patches of green on the skin; it was a hazard of Krayan life. Often these patches of algae were benign. If they were malignant, they could be removed with a low power laser. But this… this was different. She noticed a distinct sheen to her skin, as if she had covered her body with a pale green foundation. She took a mirror and examined her face. It was normal. Thank the Goddess: she was just imagining it.

But she was not.

At dawn next morning she woke up, and her mind seemed different.

It appeared to her that the sun was moving in the sky. As she lay on the bare floorboards she watched through her south-facing window as the sun rose, arced high at noon, then fell to the west into deepening cloud. Puzzled, she considered what she had seen. It had been an unusually bright day. The clouds that she had seen had raced across the sky, bubbling like froth pillows, deepening, darkening, vanishing.

She left her room and walked through the inn. It seemed empty; yet full of ghosts that whizzed by. The lamps flickered with electric rhythms that she had not noticed before.

Outside, she watched the now thickening storm clouds race across the sky. Through rents between piles of cumulus she saw the stars arc in time-lapse motion. She felt rain upon her skin, yet she saw only mist in the air and a sheen of pale water on her skin, like a sheath of the finest cellophane. Everything around her was blurred. The silhouettes of trees around her were defocused. Far away, the hands on a distant clock had vanished.

Again the sun rose. It moved quickly now, and she stood, somewhere in the Cemetery, and watched it reach its zenith then become lost in boiling cloud that appeared as if from a distant black line on the horizon. Night again. Then day, this time gloomy with no sun. Then night. Day. Night…

After a while she lost track of the motion of the heavenly bodies. Kray was grey and green: empty. She saw nobody. Around her feet the beauty of botanic movement was revealed, intricate as an urban clock laid out for her to view, leaves expanding, flowers flickering into life then dying, like spots of paint dropped from some celestial paintbrush that were absorbed into the earth. Seeds grew from wrinkled lumps on the ends of branches as if inflated by an arboreal breath.

She walked into the Garden. She had forgotten about the danger at its heart; all she saw was the vibrancy of the growing plants, the blurred purity of the green, the fertility of the soil. That soil seemed to dance at her feet. It was writhing with power.

Earth/Goddess/Elapse/Move.

She found that her memory of human things was fading.

In the Garden she found a great screen, indigo like the

eastern evening sky, furry as an antler. It was approximately square, and algae and other plant life crawled all over it, like green paint expanding on canvas. Upon it was written:

Welcome Kytanquil! Please do not touch this pyuter as you will later use it to communicate with us, bringing us the secret of immortality conferred by the Venus Heart. Go north when you have read this and meet the other Slow People. Speak with the Venus Heart, discover its secret, then return here. This pyuter has been devised so that it can read symbols left by you upon your own skin. Be concise. From our perspective, a hundred-word message will take some decades to receive. Good luck! (And please be quick.)

And Kytanquil thought: I am a Slow Person.

Her consciousness had been altered so that, like a tree, she perceived time on a different scale, a botanic scale, in which years were like hours and aeons like years.

She walked north east through a landscape temporally smoothed yet full of detail, and she understood that this had once been the future of the last city on Earth. A future she had herself considered… Not any more. She was now on a quest to escape death.

As she entered the Green Quarter she saw other Slow People. Vaguely she recalled how, long ago (or so it seemed), she had mocked them as idiots, but now she saw that their movements were graceful, swaying like the boughs of a tree, oscillating like a reed in a breeze. Yet their motions were unhuman, botanic, tiny rhythms in their fingers combining to produce limb movements. Their expressions were vacant, yet possessed a sense of profound depth, and Kytanquil found herself thinking of the complexity of bark on the bole of Kray's ancient oaks. She thought of that peaceful, archaic sense of beauty brought about by the sight of stars wheeling across the luminous sea.

Yet such memories were only just within her grasp. She was someone different now. She walked on, watching the other Slow People, noticing that they did not attempt to communicate with her. She moved ever closer to the Venus Heart.

Until she saw it.

And it was vast: a great hemisphere of sticky green gleaming amidst the blurred ruins of groves and buildings, hundreds of metres across, dark as yew, glutinous as cuckoo-spit. Kytanquil's sense of passing time was still slow enough for her to see the random decay of stone, as surrounding buildings disintegrated under the touch of wind and rain and frost. The Venus Heart, however, was constant, unchanging, a botanic entity formed from the synapses of the Venus Fly Trap and...

Something else, something technological, or so the pyutons of the Association for the Promotion of the Chlorophyll Age thought. But Kytanquil could see nothing of technology, and she realised that the pyutons, in their narcissism, had presumed the influence of humanity. The Venus Heart was natural.

So she understood that she was not obliged to return to the Garden to give her message. She was free. No reward would be offered by the Garden pyutons.

Walking around the Venus Heart she saw Slow People tending to outcrops of twisted green flesh, and after a few thousand circumnavigations she began to see a pattern in their movements. The pyutons had suspected communication to be possible with the Venus Heart; this could only happen if there was language. What sort of language?

It had to be sign language. Only a visual language could work, the audio sense being unusable. Immediately she wondered if she could learn it. For the first time she tried to communicate by gesture with one of the Slow People. After a few abortive attempts she simply copied what the other was doing, and she realised that communication with the Venus Heart was achieved by acts of gardening. This was something she could learn.

The invisible seasons passed. Years rode by on the wings of erosion. The subtler rhythms of nature – the changing heat output of the sun, variations in the atmosphere, the evolution of the landscape – impinged upon her consciousness. She absorbed them as she absorbed the language of gardening, which she learned by a combination of guesswork and gesture in the ever deep society of the Slow People.

The Venus Heart told of a richer, more profound state of consciousness, aware of long-term terrestrial rhythms, foreseeing a future in which even geological time would fold itself into the self-aware mind, so to reveal the final secrets of the Earth. This was the aim of the Venus Heart, and it had created the Slow People in order that its dream be accomplished. Alone, it was isolated. In communication it found freedom.

So Kytanquil lived in the still and depthless world between animal consciousness and plant consciousness, an aesthete of nature with a human base, yet beholden to the slow kingdom of botany. And in the end, as with everyone, her body was returned to the soil.

About the Author

Stephen Palmer is the author of fifteen novels: *Memory Seed* (Orbit 1996), *Glass* (Orbit 1997), *Flowercrash* (Wildside 2002), *Muezzinland* (Wildside 2003), *Hallucinating* (Wildside 2004), as Bryn Llewellyn, *The Rat And The Serpent* (Prime Books 2005) and *Urbis Morpheos* (PS Publishing 2010). His eighth novel, the surreal and fast-paced *Hairy London,* was published as a paperback and ebook in 2014, while the ninth, *Beautiful Intelligence,* was published in 2015 by Infinity Plus Books, as was the subsequent short novel *No Grave For A Fox.*

In 2016, Infinity Plus published his alternate-world, steampunk Factory Girl trilogy: *The Girl With Two Souls / The Girl With One Friend / The Girl With No Soul.* His novel of World War I *Tommy Catkins* was published in 2018. *The Autist* – a return to the theme of artificial intelligence – was published in 2019 by Infinity Plus Books.

His short stories have been published by Spectrum, Wildside, Solaris, NewCon Press, Unspoken Water, Mutation Press, Theakers Quarterly, Eibonvale Press, Dog Horn Press, Infinity Plus Books, Boo Books, Eco-tones, Kraxon Magazine, Woodbridge Press, Wayward Plants and Manchester Speculative Fiction.

Stephen lives and works in Shropshire, UK. Cited influences include Jack Vance, Gwyneth Jones, Gene Wolfe, Erich Fromm and James Lovelock. He is a fan of The Goons and prefers Darjeeling tea.

stephenpalmersf.wordpress.com

More New Titles from NewCon Press

Once Upon a Parsec – Edited by David Gullen

Ever wondered what the fairy tales of alien cultures are like? For hundreds of years scholars and writers have collected and retold folk and fairy stories from around our world. They are not alone. On distant planets alien chroniclers have done the same. For just as our world is steeped in legends and half-remembered truths of the mystic and the magical, so are theirs. Now, for the first time, we can share some of these tales with you…

Maura McHugh – The Boughs Withered

Kim Newman provides the introduction for this, the debut collection from accomplished Irish author Maura McHugh. Twenty tales – four of them original to the volume – which represent the best strange visions from an award-winning writer of fiction, non-fiction, comic books and plays. A series of contemporary revelations and murky pasts that draw upon the author's Irish heritage and so much more.

Simon Morden – Bright Morning Star

A ground-breaking take on first contact from scientist and novelist Simon Morden. Sent to Earth to explore, survey, collect samples and report back to its makers, an alien probe arrives in the middle of a warzone. Witnessing both the best and worst of humanity, the AI probe faces situations that go far beyond the parameters of its programming, and is forced to improvise, making decisions that may well reshape the future of a world.

Soot and Steel – edited by Ian Whates

Stories that explore London's dark underbelly but also celebrate the city's character and charm; stories that beat to the rhythm of the capital's heart. Sinister tales, ghost stories, menacing thrillers and revealing vignettes; stories of the streets, the alleyways, the sewers, the rooftops and the underground, all steeped in the essence of London's urban community, its industrial heritage, the docks, Victoriana, the Blitz, and beyond.

www.newconpress.co.uk

Rachel Armstrong – Invisible Ecologies

The story of Po, an ambiguously gendered boy who shares an intimate connection with a nascent sentience emerging within the Po delta: the bioregion upon which the city of Venice is founded. Carried by the world's oceans, the pair embark on a series of extraordinary adventures and, as Po starts school, stumble upon the Mayor's drastic plans to modernise the city and reshape the future of the lagoon and its people.

Kim Lakin-Smith – Rise

Denounced by her own father and charged with crimes against the state, Kali Titian – pilot, soldier, and engineer – is sentenced to Erbärmlich prison camp, where she must survive among her fellow inmates the Vary, a race she has been raised to consider sub-human; a race facing genocide; a race who until recently she was routinely murdering to order. A potent tale of courage against the odds and the power of hope in the face of racial intolerance.

Best of British Science Fiction 2018

Twenty-six stories, selected by editor **Donna Scott**, that represent some of the best SF published anywhere in 2018; dreamlike glimpses of pristine worlds that will destroy us before we destroy them; stories of work-based friendships, mistrust and isolation; stories of slavery given an acceptable face through beautiful voice; stories of bodily choice being made a crime; stories of rebellions we thought we'd already had but need to have again.

Ian Creasey – The Shapes of Strangers

British SF's best kept secret, Ian Creasey is one of our most prolific and successful short fiction writers, with 18 stories published in *Asimov's,* a half dozen or more in *Analog,* and appearances in a host of the major SF fiction venues. *The Shapes of Strangers* showcases Ian's perceptive and inventive style of science fiction, gathering together fourteen of his finest tales, including stories that have been selected for *Year's Best* anthologies.

NewCon Press: publishing the best in SF and fantasy

Immanion Press
Purveyors of Speculative Fiction

Love in a Time of Dragons & Other Rare Tales by Tanith Lee

'A time of dragons' might conjure the image of a fantastical medieval world, with knights dark and light, clever sorcerers and witches, doomed kings and charmed innocents. Love might seem to be very much a part of such a world, where passions rage and honour fires the blood. But the truth is that dragons come in many guises, even into modern times. As does love. In this volume of rare and uncollected tales, Tanith Lee takes up her sword to face the dragons – not only to slay them, but to see their stories reflected in the blade. For be sure they each have one to tell… ISBN: 978-1-912815-02-9 £11.99, $15.99 pbk

The Lord of the Looking Glass by Fiona McGavin

Fiona McGavin has an extraordinary talent for taking genre tropes and turning them around into something completely new, playing deftly with topsy-turvy relationships between supernatural creatures and people of the real world. 'Post Garden Centre Blues' reveals an unusual relationship between taker and taken in a twist of the changeling myth. 'A Tale from the End of the World' takes the reader into her developing mythos of a post-apocalyptic world, which is bizarre, Gothic and steampunk all at once. Following in the tradition of exemplary short story writers like Tanith Lee and Liz Williams, Fiona has a vivid style of writing that brings intriguing new visions to fantasy, horror and science fiction. ISBN: 978-1-907737-99-2, £11.99, $17.50 pbk

Songs to Earth and Sky by Storm Constantine and others

Some of the best Wraeththu Mythos writers explore the seasonal festivals of the year, dreaming up new customs, new myths, new dehara – the gods of Wraeththu. From the silent, snow-heavy forests of Megalithican mountains, through the lush summer fields of Alba Sulh, into the hot, shimmering continent of Olathe, this book brings powerful spirits and landscapes to vivid life. Nine new tales, including a novella, a novelette and a short story from Storm herself, and stories from *Wendy Darling, Nerine Dorman, Suzanne Gabriel, Fiona Lane* and *E. S. Wynn*. ISBN 978-1-907737-84-8 £11.99 $15.50 pbk

www.immanion-press.com
info@immanion-press.com